"What do you think you're doing?" Dunne demanded angrily.

"Putting the ball in your court, Mr. Holborn," Maggie said through the smile she was still aiming at the assembled magicians. "Where it belongs."

"You may not like the way I'll play it," Dunne threatened.

"You wouldn't dare make a scene," Maggie taunted him. "You'd start a riot."

"Oh, I'll start a riot all right." He grabbed her shoulders and jerked her around to face him. "What I ought to do is spank you," he said. "But I think I'll do what I want to do instead."

Maggie didn't know what she had been expecting, but it wasn't what she got.

What she got was Dunne Holborn's hot, eager lips swooping down to capture her own.

Dear Reader:

By now our new cover treatment—with larger art work—
is familiar to you. But don't forget that, in a sense, our new
cover reflects what's been happening *inside* SECOND
CHANCE AT LOVE books. We're constantly striving to
bring you fresh and original romances with unexpected
twists and delightful surprises. We introduce promising new
writers on a regular basis. And we aim for variety by publishing some romances that are funny, some that are poign-
ant, some that are "traditional," and some that take an
entirely new approach. SECOND CHANCE AT LOVE is
constantly evolving to meet your need for "something new"
in your romance reading.

At the same time, we *haven't* changed the successful edi-
torial concept behind each SECOND CHANCE AT LOVE
romance. We work hard to make sure every romance we
publish is a satisfying read. And at SECOND CHANCE AT
LOVE we've consistently maintained a reputation for being
a line of the highest quality.

So, just like the new covers, SECOND CHANCE AT LOVE
romances are satisfyingly familiar—yet excitingly different—and better than ever.

Happy reading,

Ellen Edwards

Ellen Edwards, Senior Editor
SECOND CHANCE AT LOVE
The Berkley Publishing Group
200 Madison Avenue
New York, N.Y. 10016

P.S. Do you receive our SECOND CHANCE AT LOVE
and TO HAVE AND TO HOLD newsletter? If not, be sure
to fill out the coupon in the back of this book, and we'll
send you the newsletter free of charge four times a year.

Second Chance at Love

RULES OF THE GAME

NICOLA ANDREWS

A
SECOND CHANCE AT LOVE
BOOK

Other Second Chance at Love books by
Nicola Andrews

FORBIDDEN MELODY   #139
RECKLESS DESIRE   #180
HEAD OVER HEELS   #200

RULES OF THE GAME

Copyright © 1984 by Nicola Andrews

All rights reserved. No part of this publication may be reproduced or
transmitted in any form or by any means, electronic or mechanical,
including photocopy, recording, or any information storage and re-
trieval system, without permission in writing from the publisher.

Requests for permission to make copies of any part of the work should
be mailed to: Permissions, Second Chance at Love, The Berkley Publishing Group, 200 Madison Avenue, New York, NY 10016.

First edition published September 1984

First printing

"Second Chance at Love" and the butterfly emblem are trademarks
belonging to Jove Publications, Inc.

Printed in the United States of America
Second Chance at Love books are published by
The Berkley Publishing Group
200 Madison Avenue, New York, NY 10016

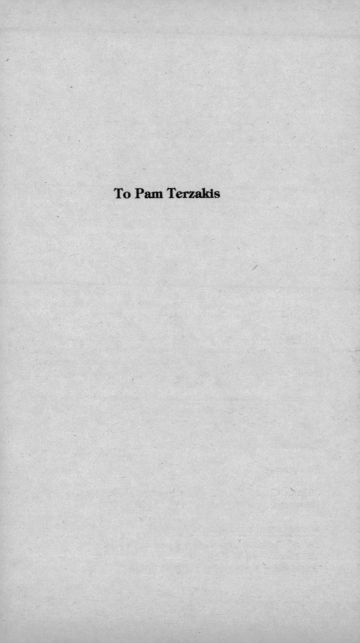

To Pam Terzakis

Chapter One

THE FIRST TIME Margaret Mary Hennessy laid eyes on Dunne Holborn, she hated him.

It wasn't just the fact that the man was so insufferably good-looking, although that would have been enough. After four years of Hamlin Marshall, Maggie knew all she ever wanted to know about good-looking men, and she didn't have a kind word to say about any of them.

She knew all she wanted to know about arrogant men, too. And Dunne Holborn was obviously an arrogant man. She could tell that much just by looking at him. His green eyes flashed. His broad shoulders were set in a way that announced better than a billboard could that he was used to getting what he wanted, when he wanted it, the way he wanted it. His thick, straight brown hair hung a little long for executive chic, and his gray flannel slacks

1

and thick white Irish fisherman's sweater were just a little too casual for proper business attire.

Clearly, Mr. Dunne Holborn didn't have to worry about the unwritten business dress code the rest of them were subject to, Maggie thought with disgust. Mr. Dunne Holborn had it made. Well, she knew all about men who had it made. They were poison.

Someone behind her yelled "Boom down left!" and she leaned over the balcony railing in front of her to get her head out of the way. The balcony was halfway up the forty-foot wall of what the Bidemeyer Trust liked to call the Main House Reception Room, and from where she stood, Maggie could see every one of the sixty people assembled to construct The Game.

Games were Maggie's business, although she hated to describe it that way. It was nearly impossible to explain that a company with over six thousand employees could do very well designing "total-environment" games for schools, universities, and organizations, but that was what Daystar did.

Some of the games were designed for use in classrooms, giving students a chance to encounter, in controlled environments, the kinds of problems they would face after graduation. There was Takeover, for instance, in which business-school students pretended to be various participants in the drama of a corporate merger. Other Daystar games, like Damsel, were just for fun. In Damsel some contestants took the roles of knights; others, magicians; others, the dragon or the damsel in distress.

Maggie wasn't sure if the game she was working on now was "just for fun" or not. It was the first special project she'd ever attempted. The L-Star Society, a group of writers, actors, editors, and motion-picture people with a strong interest in science fiction, had rented the four-hundred-acre Bidemeyer Estate and its two-hundred-and-twenty-room mansion for a week in late November. Then they had hired Daystar to set up The Game. For as long as the members of the L-Star Society remained in the confines of the Bidemeyer Estate, they would eat, sleep, dress, act, and talk as if they were residents of the planet Merival, engaged in a deadly hunt for the Dust Pirates of the black star Nathvar. Maggie had spent countless weeks designing the game, and two more preparing the preliminary setup at Bidemeyer. It had been her project, her baby. It had been her chance to prove herself as a designer. And then they had sprung Dunne Holborn on her.

Daystar *never* brought an administrator in over a chief designer, especially not in the middle of a project. Maggie had worked for the company for five years, ever since she'd left Hamlin and Los Angeles to come back to her hometown of New Haven, Connecticut, to live. She knew how the company worked because she'd made a point of familiarizing herself with its operations. She'd wanted to work at something she enjoyed, do an excellent job, and succeed spectacularly. She wanted to reaffirm her faith in a system in which hard work and talent were rewarded and in which superficialities, like looks, charm, and a commanding manner, were ignored.

She had told herself over and over that Ham's incredible success was an aberration, that most people in most places would see right through him, that it was only in the claustrophobic, incestuous subculture of the movie business that he could have succeeded at all. Not that she really blamed people for being taken in; she herself had been taken in. To the innocent girl from central Connecticut whom Maggie had been at the time, Hamlin was a dream come true. She had believed every word he told her—about himself and about his love for her.

Maggie bit her lip. How long had it taken her to realize that Hamlin Marshall was a phony, that his one ambition in life was to take as much and give as little as possible? How long had it taken her to lose respect for him? She shook her head in agitation. The change had come so gradually, she really couldn't pin it down to any one moment. There had been so many little things, little lies, little boasts, little evasions. There had been Jane Carter, who knew who the clients were and where the money was, which deals were coming down where and with whom; Jane Carter, who did Ham's work for him and never complained. Finally, Maggie had reached the point where she just couldn't stand to live in ignorance anymore. She had to know.

She could still remember the look on Ham's face when she had begun to question him. They had sat in the awful modern living room he was so fond of, and he had talked. About how he despised the "grinds." About how a smart man learned what it took to get along in the world—and it wasn't breaking your back at slave work, either. Work was for fools. You could always find someone to do the work and thank you for paying him, too. Then you could concentrate on what really mattered: personality, style, contacts.

It was a philosophy Maggie neither understood nor accepted. She'd grown up a small-town girl in a small-town family—neither rich nor poor, but with a profound respect for hard work and achievement. Ham's attitude shook her most deeply held convictions. She couldn't live in the kind of world Ham was describing or with a man who embraced it. She had filed for divorce, packed her bags, and taken a plane back East.

And landed at Daystar. Maggie almost laughed out loud. Daystar had certainly taken her mind off her ex-husband. It had given her a whole new set of problems. Daystar hired women only when it had to. It paid them less than men, promoted them much less frequently, and adamantly refused to give them any real responsibility. From the moment she first took her place behind a desk in the design department, after arduously working her way up from the typing pool, she had been fighting a running battle over the unspoken Daystar axiom that women should type, not write. And she had watched half a dozen Hamlin Marshalls move into positions of responsibility above her. Daystar's practice of discrimination was the one facet of the company she hadn't discovered in her preliminary research.

She trained her eyes on the figure on the floor below. When she'd heard they were bringing in a man to oversee her project, she had been furious at the insult to her ability. They would never have imposed an administrator on her if she were male, and she had no intention of letting them get away with it. Oh, she'd done all the necessary things. She'd written a complete report on the design and progress of The Game, included all contracts with both the L-Star Society and Bidemeyer, and sent them to Mr. Holborn's office. She'd instructed her secretary to answer any questions the man might have.

Then she'd called her lawyer.

That had been two weeks ago, before she'd ever seen Dunne Holborn. Now that she had seen him, she had a whole new cause for complaint. She gave the casually dressed figure a withering glare. Of course Holborn would look like that. Didn't they all? Smug, arrogant, lazy, talentless; it didn't matter. They got where they were going on looks, charm, and the Daystar prejudice that women weren't good enough to grace a designing board. *Men.*

A frail girl clutching a clipboard hurried up to Maggie, blushing.

"Miss Hennessy?" the girl trilled. "There's a note here about monoliths, and I don't know what they are, and I can't figure out where they're supposed to go."

Maggie turned, took the clipboard from the girl, and studied the notations on it. "Just one monolith," she said. "It's supposed to be a kind of magic rock. It goes in the exact center of the reception-room floor." Maggie wheeled around to look over the balcony again, about to point out exactly where the piece should go. Then she stopped. Dunne Holborn had disappeared. A moving crane now sat where he had been standing, and the only people on the floor were men and women in technicians' smocks. Maggie bit her lip in irritation. It made her angry enough to think he was there. It made her ready to explode to think he'd disappeared.

"Miss Hennessy?"

Maggie turned back to the nervous girl and tried to force her expression into one that conveyed professional detachment. She would just have to find Mr. Holborn later. Now that he was there, she wasn't going to let him escape with a couple of smiles, a few handshakes, and an air of somehow being secretly in charge.

She knew that routine, all right. Hamlin had been expert at it. All you had to do was exude an air of superiority and pretend to be too busy to handle trivialities, and everybody would think you were doing a wonderful job. Maggie wasn't about to let Dunne Holborn get away with it. She was going to find him, corner him, and kill him.

In the meantime she was going to do her job. She ran her hand down the left hand side of the clipboard until she came to what she wanted, then showed the line to the girl.

"The description's right here," Maggie explained. "The Monolith is a large black piece shaped a little like the Washington Monument turned upside down. It's made of obsidian, so it's heavy. You'll have to get one of the grips to move it. It's a little smaller at the bottom than at the top. What you have to do is stand it on its small end, and then—"

"And then it scratches all that nice terrazzo, and Daystar is liable for the damages."

Maggie froze. The voice that came from behind her was rich, full, deep, and more than a little sarcastic. It made her want to spit. So Mr. Dunne Holborn thought he could just walk in here and criticize her work! He hadn't even read the material she'd sent him; his remark about possible damages proved that. Of all the insufferable, high-handed, egotistical—

Maggie whirled, meaning to tell the great Mr. Dunne Holborn from the executive office just what kind of an idiot she thought he was. The words were almost out when she began to feel panic constricting her throat, and suddenly she found it difficult to breathe. Good Lord, Maggie thought in agitated dismay, he's . . . he's—

She didn't have the vocabulary to describe just what he was. *Forceful* would have been too mild. *Captivating* would have made him sound too attractive. Not that Maggie would deny that he was attractive. Frankly, the man was overwhelming. When she'd seen him from a distance, he'd looked just like any other casual, expensively dressed young man on the fast track. Up close she realized that his flannel slacks and bulky sweater did nothing to hide the well-trained muscles in his arms and legs. Dunne Holborn obviously worked on something, even if it was only his body!

Maggie shifted uneasily, feeling dizzy and certain that she was staring. She had to do something to get herself together. If she was right about Dunne Holborn—and at the moment nothing could have convinced her she wasn't—he undoubtedly realized just how much he was affecting her. He wasn't doing anything to ease her confusion, either. The way he was looking at her made her whole body tingle, and the look in his eyes—both speculative and amused—almost made her blush.

She raked her fingers through her close-cropped, curly black hair and tried to get a grip on herself. If she stood there gawking much longer, she'd lose the battle before it had even begun!

"Our contract with L-Star," she said slowly, her voice lower and less imperious than she would have wished, "states categorically that any damages incurred in the preparation or execution of The Game will be defrayed by the L-Star Society, not the company." Her voice sounded so professional, so cool, that Maggie took heart. "If you'd checked the design specifications," she continued in a louder tone, "you'd realize that the bottom of the Monolith is covered with felt to ensure against scratching."

Dunne Holborn's eyebrows shot up in surprise, and he stepped back as if to get a better look at her. Maggie felt her initial annoyance at the man return. What was he so surprised about? Maybe he didn't do any work, but surely he couldn't be under the delusion that no one else did.

"What exactly does the Monolith do?" Dunne Holborn asked.

Maggie didn't know what to say. It had been bad enough they'd sent her an administrator, but they'd sent her a complete fool as well. The man was shameless!

"What did I spend two days writing reports to you for?" she demanded, feeling something inside her snap. She knew she should play it cool, that she'd get further by outmaneuvering the man than by any attempt to bull-doze him, but she couldn't help herself. "That report I sent you contains copies of every contract, every design, the rulebook, the costume specifications, even the per-missions for the music we're using. It's got a table of contents and an index. Try carrying it around for a while. Anytime something confuses you, you can look it up."

Dunne Holborn's frown was the only indication he gave that he noticed Maggie's anger. "I haven't had time to read the report," he said equably. "I've been in Las Vegas on company business." His green eyes hardened into an appraising stare. "I assumed that you, as chief designer, would have whatever I needed to know at your fingertips."

"Then maybe I, as chief designer, should be left alone to do my job," Maggie challenged him. "If you're so *busy*"—she made *busy* sound like a different kind of four-letter word altogether—"maybe you'd be better off not interfering in my project at all."

Dunne Holborn's eyes narrowed. "Interfering? I was under the impression that special projects of this sort called for good, solid team players, Miss Hennessy, not mavericks."

"The only position Daystar offers any woman on one

of its 'teams' is mascot," Maggie spat out. She jammed her hands into the pockets of her jacket and clenched her fists, digging her nails into the soft skin of her palms. "Let me make something perfectly clear," she said. "This is the first time a woman has ever been named chief designer on a special project, and it's the first time the company has ever put an administrator over the head of a chief designer. I'm not stupid, and I'm not a meek little girl who'll keep her mouth shut and be good. I've spent the last five years being underpaid and underemployed, and I've had it."

"So you filed a lawsuit against the company," Holborn said quickly. "You ought to know that never works."

"If you want to talk about the lawsuit, you can call my lawyer," Maggie said, taking a few quick breaths to get her voice under control. "I'm trying to tell you about this project. I don't want you here, and you know it. However, I'll work with you as long as I have to. But take my word for it, Mr. Holborn, I'll be damned if I'm going to carry you. If you want to work on this game, you'd better know what you're doing, when you're doing it, and how you're doing it. If you don't, I'll take you apart. Is that understood?"

Sparks of anger flashed in Dunne Holborn's green eyes. "No wonder you've got a reputation as a troublemaker," he said frostily. "If this is the way you treat a man you've never laid eyes on before—"

"You're the beneficiary of my long and enlightening experience," Maggie said sarcastically. "Besides, I've been expecting you all day, and it's been a long, long day. Now, if you don't mind, it's after two. I'm due back at the office at four-thirty for an appointment and I'm running late. So if you'll just move out of my way, I'll get back to work."

This time the anger didn't take the form of a few sparks in his eyes or frosty tone of voice. Every muscle in the man's body seemed to contract at once, and his jaw looked about ready to crack.

"I don't care what you've got to do," he told her. "I've got to be acquainted with the particulars of this project. I need you to show me around."

For one short second Maggie hesitated. Cass Delaney, her lawyer, had made a point of telling her to do everything expected of her as long as their case was in court. Refusing to do the work required of her or neglecting to follow the orders of designated superiors could jeopardize their case. If she had any sense, she would swallow her anger and give Dunne Holborn a guided tour.

Well, she just couldn't do it. She'd been boiling since she first heard that Dunne Holborn was coming, she'd started to let off steam, and she couldn't stop now.

She gave him a wicked little grin. "Everything you need to know is in my report," she told him sweetly. "When you've read it, I'm sure you'll have a lot of questions. You can find me on the Plains of Qataq— that is, if you can *find* the Plains of Qataq." She gave him a measuring glance that started at the too-precise part in his hair and ended at the polished tips of his Gucci loafers. "Somehow," she told him, "I don't think you have much of a sense of direction."

Chapter Two

"JUST TELL ME one thing," Cass Delaney moaned, "is it bad, worse, or nearly impossible?"

Maggie poured too much cream into her coffee, scowled at the cup, then decided to live with her mistake and drink the stuff. She'd walked out of the main house at Bidemeyer in a state of euphoric self-righteousness, only to be hit almost immediately by cold winds and colder thoughts. By the time she'd spent an hour at the northwest corner of the estate—now known as the Plains of Qataq—she was in a state of self-accusatory panic, sure that she had ruined everything. She would lose her job, lose her case, and find herself broke and unemployed before she knew it. She had to go back and apologize. She had to!

She hadn't been able to. By the time she got back to

the main house, Dunne Holborn had disappeared again, and she found herself standing aimlessly in the foyer, biting her nails and getting in the way of three technicians struggling with the lavender strobe lights. Since she knew very little about lighting, she had been unable to help them with their problems. She'd ended up feeling like an incompetent fool, and that had made her even more depressed.

That's when she'd decided to call Cass, her longtime friend and now lawyer, and set up a meeting at the True Blue Coffee Shop. Thank heaven for the True Blue, Maggie had thought as she climbed into her car for the hour-long trip from the Bidemeyer Estate to New Haven. It wasn't on company property, which made it suitable for a meeting with Cass, but it was directly across from Daystar's main building, on Elm Street, which meant she could watch the door for signs of Dunne Holborn. If she saw him, she would just have to run right out and corral him. She had the feeling that the sooner she made her apologies, the better.

Maggie took a long gulp of her overcreamed coffee and said, "I didn't actually hit him."

Cass dug her short, stubby fingers into her blazing red hair and groaned again. "I can't believe this," she wailed. "I spent an entire Saturday afternoon telling you what you had to do, what you had to say, how you had to behave. And now you do *this*."

"I couldn't help myself," Maggie protested. "I've been going crazy about this whole situation for weeks, long before we decided to file suit. It's just so infuriating. And then in walks this—this *man*, standing around, acting as if he owns the earth, and criticizing me when he doesn't even know what I'm doing. I came apart. In more ways than one."

Cass gave her a murderous glare. "What's that supposed to mean?" she asked. "In more ways than one."

"I don't know." Maggie sighed, thinking of the strange strangling feeling she'd had when she'd first encountered

Dunne Holborn up close. "Cass, please," she begged, "I'm just so confused. It's been a terrible day, I've been a complete idiot, I'm still angry—I don't know what I'm doing!"

"I should have killed you back in grammar school," Cass erupted. "Back in the fifth grade, when we had that fight out on Orange Street after school. I had the chance; I should have taken it."

"If you had, Bobby Fitzgerald and Tommy Murphy would have killed *you* when you made dates with both of them for your senior prom. I got you out of that one."

"Sister Cecilia got me out of that one," Cass said. "She's the one who grounded Bobby Fitzgerald for climbing into the convent kitchen and trying to steal a pie."

"Who do you think gave Bobby Fitzgerald the idea?"

Cass groaned. "Maggie, for heaven's sake, we're not in grammar school now. We're grown women, we're both over twenty-eight, and we've just done a very serious thing: We've filed suit against the company you work for for violations of the Civil Rights Act and the Connecticut Fair Employment Practices Act. If you don't win this case, you're going to be virtually unemployable."

"I know," Maggie said miserably.

"I counseled you to start a class action rather than an individual suit," Cass reminded her. "Daystar is vulnerable to that, and we wouldn't have had to depend so much on you. We'd just have had to prove that there was a pattern of discrimination."

"Which there is," Maggie said quickly.

"I know there is," Cass said. "But you didn't want a class action; you wanted an individual suit. So we filed one. But, Maggie, you can't go around blowing off steam every time you feel like it. And if you're as attracted to that man as I think you are, you'd better be the only one who ever knows it!"

Shocked, Maggie stared at her friend. "I'm not attracted to that man," she protested violently. "I couldn't possibly be attracted to a man like Dunne Holborn."

"No?" Cass asked shrewdly. "I've known you a long time, Maggie Hennessy, and I've been around a little on my own. I know the signs when I see them. We're sitting here, theoretically discussing your professional future, and all you can think about is *him*. I can tell."

Maggie shook her head vigorously. It was true that Dunne Holborn had a strange—and strangely over-whelming—effect on her, but Maggie was certain she couldn't be attracted to him. Not in the way Cass meant, surely. The idea was ridiculous.

"He reminds me of Ham," she explained virtuously, "and you know how I feel about him."

"You were in love with him once," Cass said quietly.

"And by the time I left him I hated him," Maggie said. "I had good reason to: He was a cheat and a liar. This Holborn character is exactly the same type." She hesitated at the half lie. No, she thought, Holborn wasn't exactly the same type; there was a subtle difference, something she couldn't quite pin down. She dismissed the thought. Whatever the difference was, she was sure it didn't make any difference. "Maybe that's why I'm so upset. They didn't just send me an administrator; they sent me a pretty boy who doesn't know his rear end from his elbow!"

Cass nodded thoughtfully. "Yes," she said slowly. "If he really is what you say he is, it may give us a handle."

"Of course he is what I say he is," Maggie insisted. "I may not have gone to law school, Cass Delaney, but I did go to California. I know the type when I see it!"

"Let me check it out," Cass soothed. "I just keep getting the feeling I've heard the name Dunne Holborn before. Heaven only knows where." She started to dig her purse out of her oversize tote. "I'll go back to the office and see if I can find anything on this guy. In the meantime, you go back there"—she pointed across the street at the Havelock Building, where Daystar's design offices were located—"and *try* to have a normal, uneventful rest of the day."

When Maggie got off the elevator at the fourteenth floor, she found Clare Dobson, the round-figured, white-haired, pink-faced little woman who was general secretary for the design department, standing in the hall, a rectangular package under her arm and a puzzled expression on her face. Maggie gave the woman a quick hello and started to hurry past, when Clare seemed to snap into consciousness.

"Miss Hennessy," the older woman trilled, "this box—" Clare stopped, shook her head, and stood a little straighter. "Maybe I ought to start from the beginning," she said. "There's a man waiting for you. He's dressed in a metallic green jump suit and a helmet like those old-fashioned deep-sea divers used to wear, and he's got things coming out of his head."

"*What?*"

"He says he's got an appointment," Clare sighed. "I wanted to call the police or maybe Mr. Carstairs over in marketing—Mr. Carstairs is almost seven feet tall; he could take care of a little man—but the little man says his name is Robert Horvath, and you do have an appointment with a Robert Horvath for four-thirty, so I didn't know—"

"It's all right," Maggie interrupted, not entirely sure it was. "I've never met Mr. Horvath, but he's supposed to be the representative of one of the regional groups of the L-Star Society. Maybe he's here with some, uh, costume suggestions."

Clare snorted. "Maybe he's just plain crazy," she said tartly. "Why I didn't go to work for a nice mill company somewhere, I just don't know. People running around in space suits, people hanging up the phone in my ear. Not that it's going to do me any good to complain about Mr. Holborn, of course. I'm only a secretary, but still—"

"Mr. Holborn called and hung up on you?" Maggie

cut in weakly, feeling the familiar roiling in her stomach. Maggie must have infuriated him even more than she'd thought. "Did he say what he was angry about?" she asked Clare tentatively.

"He didn't say anything," Clare pronounced stoutly. "He just called up, asked if you were in, was told you weren't, and hung up. Not so much as a thank you. *Fifteen times.*"

"Mr. Holborn called fifteen times?" This was getting worse by the minute. What could he have to say to her that was so important it required him to call fifteen times? "You're fired?" Or did he just want to give her a little of what she'd given him this morning? Maggie could feel her head begin to ache. "I was out at Bidemeyer, and so was he," she explained unnecessarily and lamely. "If he wanted me, he could have found me."

"I don't know about that," Clare said. "All I know is that he called and called and called, and then he said he wasn't going to call anymore. Then he sent this." Clare held out the box.

Maggie stared down at it, barely managing to stifle her urge to ask Clare if it was ticking. *Now* what? The package wasn't the right size for papers or books. It was too large to be a cassette tape or a Dictaphone reel. What could Dunne Holborn possibly be sending her?

"If you want to know what's in it," Clare said, "you're going to have to open it."

"I do want to know what's in it," Maggie admitted. "At least, I think I do. Do you think Mr. Holborn would be capable of sending a—well, I mean, something booby-trapped?"

Clare fixed Maggie with a knowing look, her eyes gleaming. "I've been around here longer than you have, and as far as I'm concerned, Mr. Holborn is capable of anything."

"Right," Maggie said. She certainly didn't want to pursue that line of conversation. She was too upset and confused already. She looked furtively at the door of the waiting room. "Do you think you can hold off Mr. Horvath for a few minutes?" she asked Clare. "I'd like to slip in the side door and open this thing before I see him."

"You go right ahead," Clare said. "I'll go back to my desk and concentrate on inventing a ray gun." She stalked off in the direction of the waiting-room door. Halfway there she stopped, turned, and gave Maggie a long, appraising stare. "Is it true what they're saying? You're suing the company?"

Maggie nodded.

"Good," Clare Dobson said. "Take the bastards for all they're worth."

Maggie watched the usually motherly old woman with something akin to shock. Everybody seemed to be going crazy today! Who would ever have expected that dear Mrs. Dobson had so much hostility in her? Maybe Cass was right, Maggie thought. Maybe she should have filed for class action.

Maggie looked down at the package in her hands. If she was going to open it and still get to Mr. Horvath in time, she was going to have to move fast. She made her way down the corridor to the side door to the design department, slipped inside, and hurried through the narrow corridors to her office. Once inside she opened the thin blinds that covered her old-fashioned mullioned windows and sat very carefully behind her desk. Then she positioned the box exactly in the center of the desk blotter and stared at it.

Come on, she chided herself. Of course it isn't a bomb. You've just had a bad day. You're losing your perspective.

Then she thought of Dunne Holborn's smoldering eyes, his clenched jaw, the hard, unyielding muscles beneath the civilized restraint of his gray flannel pants. She felt a shiver of fear—and of something else. She could almost feel the man there beside her, his green eyes boring into hers. Something about the image made her feel ready to melt, to give up consciousness, to . . .

Stop it! she told herself viciously. She was being ridiculous. She'd met the man exactly once. She'd never even heard of him before today. Besides, she knew his type, and she was no longer susceptible. It was just the anxiety over the state of her career that was getting to her, that was all. There was nothing more complicated in her reaction to Dunne Holborn.

With the kind of fury she wished she could apply to the whole problem of her life at that moment, she attacked the brown wrapping paper covering the package. She tore it to shreds. When she was done, she found an elegant gold cardboard box.

The gold box made her uneasy. It was as if Dunne Holborn were clairvoyant, as if there were something secret, magic, even frightening about him, something she could neither compete with nor defeat.

It's only Godiva chocolates, she told herself. Anyone can send Godiva chocolates. It doesn't mean anything.

She pulled the lid off the box and picked up the card that had been enclosed.

You were right, it read. *A good executive doesn't make comments or decisions without having all the facts. I apologize. D.H.*

She laid the note aside. Dunne Holborn had apologized. That was disturbing—it upset all her judgments of him—but she was going to have to deal with that later. Right now she was faced with something far more difficult to swallow.

The gold box was full of raspberry creams, nothing but raspberry creams. Two pounds of them. How could Dunne Holborn have known she practically had a mania for Godiva raspberry creams? How could he have known it was the only kind of candy she ate?

Things got better. Even though it was late in the afternoon, Maggie had a lot of work on her desk. It took her mind off Dunne Holborn, raspberry creams, even the scene she'd made that morning. Usually she was irritated when she returned to the office after a full day in the field and found her desk awash with papers. Today she welcomed the deluge. She would have welcomed King Kong if he could divert her attention from the persistent problem of Dunne Holborn.

Robert Horvath wasn't King Kong, but he certainly helped. Clare's description of his costume had been an understatement. Horvath was decked out as the original little green man from Mars, except, according to him, he wasn't from Mars. He was from the planet Alzibar.

"The Alzibarians joined L-Star four years ago," he explained when he was finally seated across from her in the ancient wingbacked chair that was the only visitor's seat in her office. "We've established a colony just outside Boston, in Somerville. We feel very comfortable there. The climate is so much like that of our home planet."

Maggie stared curiously at the little man. "Do you really go around dressed like that, uh, all the time?" she asked.

"Oh, no!" Horvath replied blithely. "Our people aren't rich, Miss Hennessy. They have jobs to go to. It would hardly be appropriate."

"Hardly," Maggie agreed.

"But we do like to revert to type, you see, when we come to conventions," Horvath went on. "That's why I had to see you. I've looked over the game plan you sent out for the November convention, and, well, we're not there!"

"Not there?" Maggie asked blankly.

"There are no Alzibarians on the planet you've created, Miss Hennessy. No Alzibarians at all! What will we do?"

"Ah," Maggie said, light dawning on her. She rummaged around in her desk, looking for the specifications for Bidemeyer and telling herself it would be rude to laugh out loud. After all, she had been warned about this sort of thing when she was first put on the project. All kinds of harmless crazies came to science fiction conventions. There were Trekkies, who came dressed as various characters in the old *Star Trek* television show. There were Luke Skywalkers and Ewoks and Solarians, who were devoted to the characters in *Star Wars*. Why shouldn't Mr. Horvath and his friends invent their own planet and settle down to live there?

"I think we can fix you up," she said easily, "if you'll just give me some information on the Alzibarians. How many of you are there? What are your special powers or limitations?"

"I've got it all right here." Horvath took a sheaf of papers from what looked like a kangaroo pouch in his shiny green suit. Then he settled down in his chair and gave her a big grin. "I knew you'd be able to help us," he confided. "As soon as Mr. Holborn gave me your name, I knew you'd be the one who'd ensure the rights of the Alzibarians!"

By the time Maggie had finished the exhausting process of changing an element in the game—calling L-Star for permission, changing the character list, filing the specifications for the Alzibarians in triplicate—it was after seven. Clare Dobson had gone home, and it was starting to snow. Maggie stood up, stretched, and leaned her head against a windowpane to look out at the town of New Haven below. From this window she could see almost all of the Old Campus of Yale University. Maggie had decided long ago that whoever had designed the Yale campus had to be as unusual a man in his way as Robert Horvath was in his. Certainly there wasn't any rational reason for building a moat into the campus of a modern university.

She looked back at her desk and frowned. She really should get more work done before calling it a day. That funny little man and his Alzibarians had taken up her whole evening, and she still had three sets of designs to

recheck before going out to Bidemeyer the next day.
After what she'd said to Dunne Holborn that morning,
she didn't dare show up at work knowing less than everything about the projects for the day.

At the thought of Dunne her gaze traveled to the gold
box she had shoved almost out of sight on top of the
filing cabinet. Her frown deepened. She didn't have to
remind herself that she had Dunne to think about as well
as her work. In a subliminal sense she'd been thinking
about him all day. It seemed she could call up the vision
of those challenging green eyes at will, and when she
did, her skin began to feel hot and her heart began to
beat much too rapidly. The knowledge that he would be
at the site the next morning, probably hanging around
her all day, practically made her feel faint.

No doubt Cass was right, Maggie decided; she probably was attracted to Dunne Holborn, even if she didn't
want to be. Maybe she was one of those women who
inevitably found themselves drawn to the wrong kind of
man.

The thought disturbed her so much that she began to
bustle around her office, picking up papers and shoving
them into the canvas tote she used instead of a briefcase,
unhooking her coat from the coat stand. She paused when
she came to the gold Godiva box, then forced herself to
leave it where it was. Just because she was more affected
by Dunne Holborn than she would have liked didn't mean
she had to give in to that attraction. She could at least
make an effort to get the man out of her mind.

She let herself into the corridor and locked her office
door behind her. Then she headed for the waiting room.
The side door was really more convenient for getting to
the elevator bank she preferred, but at that time of night
it would undoubtedly be locked. She didn't want to go
through all those dark corridors, only to find herself
stranded.

She was unlocking the waiting-room door when she
realized the lights in there were on. She paused, her hands

on the unturned key. It wasn't like Clare to leave the lights blazing when she left work. The woman was much too conscientious for that.

Maggie turned her key and slipped into the waiting room, squinting in the sudden harsh light.

"Is anyone here?" she asked tentatively, suddenly remembering the stories she'd heard about thieves sneaking through the building at night, stealing typewriters and sometimes even computer terminals.

There was a cough and a faint shuffling sound to her right.

"I'm here," Dunne Holborn said. "I was beginning to think you never went home."

Chapter Three

I'M NOT GOING to panic, Maggie thought. I'm not going to panic, I'm not going to panic, I'm—

Oh, to hell with it. I'll panic.

She turned, as slowly as she was able, to look at Dunne Holborn. "Did you have to sneak up on me like that?" she asked him. "I've been hearing all these stories about thieves in the building. I thought you were a desperado."

"I'm sorry." Dunne sounded sincere. "I got here just as Clare Dobson was leaving. She said you were working, so I thought—"

"You thought you'd scare me to death and solve your whole problem," Maggie said a little shakily. "Well, congratulations—you nearly succeeded."

"I thought I'd ask you to dinner," Dunne said, looking amused. "However, I'm beginning to think I should have gone home. We don't seem to have much luck getting off on the right foot, do we?"

Maggie chuckled in spite of herself. "No, we don't," she admitted. Then she hastened to add, "But about this morning: It was all my fault, and I do apologize for it."

Dunne waved dismissively. "Don't worry about it. I've been in this business long enough to know that someone in your position—someone who's had a superior foisted on them—isn't usually in too good a mood about it. And I should never have criticized you without reading your report. *I* apologize for *that*." He looked her over curiously. "Did you get my package?" he asked.

"Oh, yes," Maggie assured him, thinking about the gold box on top of her filing cabinet. "How did you know I like raspberry creams?"

"Not just raspberry creams," Dunne said, grinning. "Godiva raspberry creams. I've got my sources, Miss Hennessy"—he frowned, as if an unpleasant thought had crossed his mind—"although sometimes those sources aren't good enough," he said cryptically. Then he broke into a smile. "So how about dinner? You be the woman, I'll ply you with wine and song, and by the end of the evening maybe we'll be able to stand each other enough to work together. Then we can both settle down and give L-Star the service it deserves."

"Well . . ." Maggie hesitated, frantically trying to decide what Cass would say about such a development. Cass's three big rules for the success of the pending case were: Maintain a pleasant attitude, do everything you're asked to do, and don't do anything that may be construed as unprofessional. Maggie had a feeling that a social dinner with Dunne Holborn could get very unprofessional very fast. On the other hand, turning him down might seem uncooperative.

She looked speculatively at Dunne. He was as overwhelming as ever, but there was something about his attitude this evening that made him less frightening than he had been when she first saw him. Besides, people had business dinners all the time. It didn't mean anything.

And she *wanted* to have dinner with him.

"All right," she finally decided. Then, getting a brilliant idea, she brightened. "I even know the perfect restaurant. It's one of my favorites in the area."

"Lead on," Dunne said cheerfully. "I'm always looking for new places."

"It's quite a drive," Maggie admitted. "All the way out to Upper Stepney. But it's worth it."

"This," Dunne Holborn said as they pulled into the parking lot, "is a hot dog stand."

Maggie looked fondly at the battered green facing of Foot Long Hotdogs. "It's not just a hot dog stand," she told him. "It's *the* hot dog stand. My grandparents used to bring me here. My brother and his wife bring my nieces and nephews here now. I haven't had a chance to get out here in ages."

With what seemed like a great deal of ado, Dunne turned off the idling engine of his Alfa Romeo and sat back in his black-leather upholstered seat to look at her. "Has anyone ever told you you're a very strange woman?" he asked. "Here I am, offering you an unlimited-expense-account dinner, and instead of pointing me in the direction of a fifteen-dollar steak, you bring me here."

"I like it here." Maggie toyed with the handle of her door. The Alfa Romeo had surprised her when she first saw it, and it still made her uncomfortable. Such cars cost tens of thousands of dollars. Surely, no matter what Dunne Holborn was making, he couldn't afford a car like that. Was maintaining an image that important to him? She found herself thinking that there must be another explanation for it.

Maggie pulled on the door handle and let herself out, knowing she would have to watch herself. Dunne Holborn was getting to her. She was letting him charm her into thinking he was different, and she knew that wasn't true. She'd had ample evidence of what he was really like that morning. His apology didn't change that. She was willing to admit he might be more polite than Ham, but he was still an arrogant, ruthless, gets-what-he-wants-when-he-wants-it man, and she didn't want any part of it.

She waited while he unfolded himself from the small car and stood to shake out the creases in his pants. Foot Long Hotdogs was far out on a country road, and its parking lot was surrounded by hedges. It was easy to feel as though they were on a different planet.

Thinking of different planets made Maggie think of Robert Horvath, and she giggled.

"Now what?" Dunne demanded.

"I was thinking of one Robert Horvath, Alzibarian. He told me you sent him," Maggie said.

"Yeah." Dunne grinned sheepishly. "I've known Bob Horvath for a while. He's a fixture at these conventions. I hope he didn't upset you."

"It's Clare Dobson you ought to worry about," Maggie said. "Horvath showed up in a shiny green suit and a diver's helmet with antennae sticking out of it, and Clare was ready to quit."

"Quit?" Dunne frowned, and Maggie again had the feeling he was thinking of something that seriously bothered him. Then he turned away and pointed to the stand. "What can I get you? I said I'd buy you dinner, and I'm going to."

"Two with everything," Maggie said promptly.

"*Two* with everything?" Dunne cast an appraising glance over Maggie's slim figure. "Stranger and stranger," he declared, marching away.

Instead of going back to the car, Maggie walked over to the picnic tables, cleared a thin layer of snow from the top of one with the sleeve of her coat, and spread it with sections of the newspaper she was carrying in her tote bag. Then she climbed up and sat down to wait for Dunne.

When Dunne returned, he gave the newspapers an uncertain look but climbed up and sat down beside her without complaining. For a few moments they ate in silence. Maggie looked at the dusting of snow and the trees and the night, thinking about all those Sunday afternoons of her childhood when the whole family would come out of church and pile into the old Plymouth station wagon and drive there for lunch. Her parents and her grandparents had all been alive then, and they had been what Maggie now knew was unusually close. She had been a fool to run off to California, thinking that "life" was only to be found in the bright lights of big cities and the frenzied music of smoky discotheques.

She had fallen into a reverie of reminiscence when Dunne stood up, aimed a balled-up napkin at a nearby trash barrel, and executed a perfect hook shot. When he sat down again, his hands were in his pockets and there was a gentle, searching look in his eyes that made Maggie's heart lurch.

"You know," he teased her in a soft voice, "if you're going to get pensive on me, you ought to do it out loud. I'm interested in anything you've got to say."

Maggie didn't know if it was the concern in Dunne's eyes or the caring tone of his voice, but something about him suddenly made her feel that here was a kindred spirit, a mind and heart she could confide her deepest secrets to. A moment later she was numb with shock. What was she thinking of? Ham had been good at reading people's emotions, too. It was a necessary talent for a man of ruthless ambition. She of all people should know better than to be taken in by a sincere smile and a soft look.

She scooted away from him, wanting to create some physical as well as emotional space.

"I thought we were going to talk about the project," she said nervously.

Dunne fixed her with a look that was so frankly speculative, Maggie was afraid he was going to pursue the subject of her ruminative lapse. Then he looked away, stretched out his legs, and began rocking back and forth in the cold.

"I'm not too sure 'talk about the project' is the right way to put it," he said slowly. "'Reassure you' may be more like it."

"Reassure me?"

"That I'm not going to interfere," he explained. "That I'm not going to come in and rearrange everything. You go ahead and do what you think is right. I'll just be there to watch and make suggestions if you get into any difficulties."

Maggie stared. She'd met a lot of men like Dunne Holborn in her life, but never one who was so blatant about it.

"So you're just going to stand around and watch," she taunted, feeling the anger rising like hot needles behind her eyes. Of all the arrogant, insufferable— "Then what happens?" she asked him, unable to hide her sarcasm. "You go back to your boss and tell him what a wonderful job you've been doing? You sit on your rear end for the next four weeks and then take credit for everything I've done?"

"What?" Dunne asked, sounding genuinely surprised.

Maggie couldn't stand his pretense of innocence. It was all very well for Cass to talk about keeping one's cool and approaching every problem like a professional; Cass didn't have to put up with people like Dunne Holborn. Maggie jumped down from the picnic table and began flapping her arms against the cold.

"It's bad enough that you're here," she told Dunne furiously. "It's worse that you don't seem to want to read reports. But to announce that I'm going to be doing all the work for the rest of this project when you know your position is going to land you with all the glory, and to expect me to *swallow* it—"

"Will you slow down?" Dunne interrupted. He, too, had gotten down from the table and was now standing beside her. He grabbed her roughly by the shoulders and forced her to stand still. "I thought you wanted free rein on this project!"

"I want responsibility for this project," Maggie said coldly. "The way it is now, I'll have the responsibility in fact, you'll have it in name, and when it's over, you're the one who'll look like a hero. I'll get as much recognition as a secretary!"

Dunne pulled her close to him and peered intently into her eyes. "You're crazy," he said finally. "You're a raving lunatic. I'd think this was the perfect situation—"

"Perfect for whom?" Maggie asked, jerking herself free of him. She wrapped her arms around her chest and glared at him. "It's certainly perfect for you, Mr. Holborn. In fact, it's a dream come true."

"But, Maggie—" Dunne started.

"It's Ms. Hennessy," Maggie said imperiously.

"Ms. Hennessy," he said through gritted teeth, "I'm going to tell you once, and I'm not going to tell you again: You're making a mistake."

"You're the one who's making a mistake," Maggie said. She looked down at the half-eaten hot dog in her hand and frowned. Her temper had cooled to the point where she was simply angry, not blindly furious, and it occurred to her that the best possible move at that moment would be to get away from Dunne. She chucked the remains of her dinner into the trash barrel and headed for the car. "Let's get out of here," she called to him over her shoulder. "Obviously this meeting is not accomplishing what it was supposed to."

He stopped her just before she reached the door, placed his hands on her shoulders, and turned her around to face him, doing so with such force that she didn't dare resist. His eyes were dark and serious and half amused, which made her distinctly and, she was sure, unnecessarily upset. The emotional tone of the situation had shifted in a way she couldn't quite define. She no longer felt in control of herself or the scene.

"I'm going to give you one more chance, Ms. Hennessy. Are you *sure* you don't want to hear this explanation?"

Maggie drew a deep breath. She was not going to let this man manipulate her. If she gave in to him now, he'd spend the rest of the project walking all over her. She had no intention of ever letting a man walk all over her again.

"What I want now," she told him, "is to go home and get some work done. In peace."

He inclined his head. "Done. But don't say I didn't warn you."

Then he walked around the car to the driver's door, opened it, and got in.

It was a long, silent ride home, and a tense one. Maggie couldn't help noticing the difference in their moods. She was still anxious and upset and a little depressed, as she was after any display of anger. Dunne seemed completely unconcerned. He whistled his way through Upper Stepney, hummed through Orange, and pulled up in front of her house in West Haven, singing a song about leprechauns. Leprechauns! Maggie hated leprechauns the way only a very American child growing up in a very Irish neighborhood could hate leprechauns. She despised them.

Dunne pulled into the driveway of her small two-family house and switched off the car engine.

"If you'll sit still," he told her, "I'll get out, help you from the car, and see you to your door. The perfect gentleman."

"Don't bother—" Maggie started to say. It was too late. Dunne was already tromping around to her side of the car.

"Step this way," he said as he opened her door. "Your keys, madam?"

Maggie took her keys from her purse and slapped them into his hand. "This really isn't necessary," she told him. "I find my way home after work every night of my life."

"Do you own the house or rent?" Dunne asked pleasantly.

"I own it. Or I own most of it. The bank owns some of it."

"I see. Then you rent out that side"—he pointed to the half of the front porch where seven small bicycles leaned against the railing—"to defray the mortgage. An investor. I've always admired a woman with a head for investments."

"That side of the house," Maggie said, beginning to feel a little breathless, "is rented by the O'Shaughnessys. They've got too many children and they've had too much trouble to rent for any more than I charge."

"An investor with a heart!" Dunne exclaimed, swinging around to lean against her closed front door and look down at her. "Even better," he said with an arch of his eyebrows.

Maggie gave up. "If you're going to let me in, let me in," she said wearily. "I don't know what you think you're up to now, but I'm too tired to hear it."

Dunne didn't move. "When I originally asked you to dinner," he said slowly, "I had a slightly different agenda planned. I didn't think we'd start out discussing business. I thought we'd begin with . . . other things."

"What other things?" Maggie asked suspiciously. Dunne was turning the full force of his charm on her, and it was having its effect. Her skin had begun to tingle and her heart to pound, and she knew if she stayed there much longer, the staunch defenses she had erected against this man would begin to crumble. Damn his deep green eyes! He was entirely too good at this sort of thing. Now that she'd met Dunne Holborn, she was inclined to think Hamlin Marshall had been an amateur.

"You shouldn't be allowed loose on the street," she told him when he didn't answer. "You're dangerous."

"Very," he admitted gravely. He leaned closer to her, and for one breathless minute Maggie thought he was going to kiss her. Something very much like fire spread through her muscles, leaving her weak. Then he stepped back, and the moment was over.

"Before I open the door, I'd like to make a couple of things perfectly clear," he told her.

"What?" she asked, fighting for breath.

"You think I'm going to come in, goof off, and then steal your thunder. That's your assessment of what's happening now on the L-Star project."

"Yes," Maggie said stoutly.

"You think I need to use your work to further my career."

"Exactly."

"Just wanted to be sure." He put the key into the lock, turned it, and shoved the door open. "I should offer to come in and check the place for burglars," he said cheerfully, "but I've got a feeling you'd take it the wrong way."

Maggie hurried past him and switched on both the hall and porch lights. "I don't need you to check for burglars," she told him, cursing the way her nervousness could be heard in her voice. Why couldn't she manage to remain cool and calm where Dunne Holborn was concerned? Why did his every change of mood buffet her like a strong wind, tilting her off balance? "I'm fine," she said. "Really."

"I'm sure you are. Good night, Ms. Hennessy."

"Good night," she said with profound relief.

Dunne hopped down the three small porch steps, then stopped at the pavement. "Pick you up tomorrow morning at seven-thirty," he called out.

"Oh, no you won't!" Maggie protested, hurrying after him to the edge of the porch.

"Yes I will!" Dunne shouted as he wedged himself into the Alfa Romeo. "We left your car back in New Haven."

The engine roared to life, the exhaust pipe sputtered, and he was backing out of her driveway and pointing the car in the direction of Orange.

Maggie leaned back against the doorjamb and stared at the porch ceiling. "I'm going to kill him," she muttered. "Before this project is over, I'm going to kill the man."

That was when the phone started to ring.

Chapter Four

MAGGIE AWOKE THE next morning to a two-inch coating of snow on the ground, a fierce backache, and the realization that she had spent the night on her ancient, lumpy living-room sofa. She should have given the thing to her brother Jim, she thought sleepily as she twisted and arched to get the cricks out of her spine. She should have taken it to the dump. Just because it was Grandmother Foley's was no reason to—

The phone. Maggie shook her head. The phone was ringing.

Suddenly everything came back to her: Dunne's car pulling out of her driveway, then Cass's excited, exasperated voice on the phone. "Don't you know who Dunne Holborn is?" Cass had demanded. "I thought I'd heard the name before. I can't believe we've been so stupid!"

Maggie bolted to her feet and ran toward the wall phone in the kitchen. After she'd hung up on Cass the night before, she'd been too upset and furious even to think of sleep. She'd paced for hours, thinking over the events of the day and trying to come to some kind of a decision about what to do. All she'd managed to do was get herself thoroughly upset. Then she'd fallen asleep on that damned couch. Now she had a backache as well as a headache to blame on Dunne Holborn, she thought. She was being unreasonable, but she didn't care. Every time she thought of Cass's phone call, she wanted to ax-murder someone. Of all the people she knew, Dunne Holborn was the best candidate for violent slaughter.

The clock on the kitchen wall said seven. Maggie blinked at it. Seven? *Seven?* Good Lord. If it wasn't Dunne on the phone, calling to say he'd be late, she was going to have to run like a track star to be ready by the time he got here.

She reached the phone, grabbed the receiver, and barked "Hello!" in her least friendly voice. The receiver somehow slipped to her shoulder. She snatched it up again and pressed it to her ear. "Hello?" she tried again.

"Miss Hennessy?" Clare Dobson's voice sounded reedy and frail. "Miss Hennessy, I know it's early, and I hope I didn't wake you, but I got to the office just a few minutes ago—I had some extra work to do for Mr. Demming in Sales—and I thought I'd come in and get it over with while I had the chance, and—"

"Are you all right?" Maggie interrupted anxiously. The more Clare talked, the odder she sounded. "Has something happened?"

"I tried to call Mr. Holborn," Clare said virtuously. "He wasn't home."

Maggie groaned. Dunne was probably already on his way to her house. He might even be early. Now, if she could only find out what Clare wanted and get off the phone . . .

"Under the circumstances," Clare said, "I thought I'd better call you."

"Under what circumstances?"

Clare coughed politely. "Well"—she hesitated—"you see . . . I mean, well, I think they're holding a sit-in. The people in the hall, that is."

"What people in the hall?" Maggie asked frantically.

"The *Pter-o-to-peths,"* Clare carefully enunciated, sounding as if she were reading the name from a piece of paper. "I don't know who they are," she said carefully, "but they're dressed up like old-time magicians. You know what I mean: robes, dunce caps, that sort of thing."

Maggie groaned again. First Dunne Holborn, then Robert Horvath, now this. She just wished her mind weren't so foggy. When she was as tired as she was at that moment, everything tended to get a little unclear, and she found it difficult to think. Obviously there was more to this special-projects business than she had anticipated. She reminded herself that she had been warned. Everyone had told her that being chief designer on a special-projects game meant being as much an administrator as a designer. Everyone had told her that science fiction conferences were full of crazies. She should have expected that sort of thing. Of course, she couldn't have expected Dunne Holborn, but she'd deal with him later. She'd deal with him when he got there.

"Listen, Clare," she said, "hold tight, don't panic, and I'll be there as soon as I can. Are they blocking anything?"

"The door to the waiting room," Clare replied. "I don't think they're going to move, either."

"Don't try to make them," Maggie advised. "Send one of the girls to stand in the lobby by the elevators and another to stand by the elevator bank upstairs. Have them direct as many people as possible to the side door, so there won't be a backup. This early there shouldn't be too much of a problem."

"This early the girls aren't here yet."

"Then you take the first callers," Maggie said. "And don't worry. I'll be there as soon as I can."

Clare made a grunt that sounded like assent, and Maggie hung up and looked at the kitchen clock. Seven-ten. Ten minutes for a shower, ten minutes to dress. It was tight, but she'd make it. She had to.

She headed toward the back of the house at a trot. When she got herself together, she knew exactly what she was going to do. She was going to dump this whole problem into the lap of the great, the incomparable, the manipulative Mr. Dunne Holborn.

It would serve him right.

She was tying the blue and red embroidered sash at the waist of her blue jumper when she heard the purr of the Alfa Romeo's engine in the drive. She leaned a little closer to the beveled mirror that stood at the back of her cherrywood vanity table—another inheritance from Grandmother Foley—and checked to make sure everything was in place. Then she smiled. Everything was not only in place, it was perfect. Under the jumper she wore a soft turtleneck sweater that made her high-cheekboned face look delicate and exotic. The blue of the jumper made her eyes look even bluer, and the sash displayed her tiny waist dramatically. She was going to have a good time with Mr. Dunne Holborn that day, Maggie decided. She'd show him what happened to people who tried to manipulate *her*.

The doorbell rang. Maggie fluffed her short black curls with the tips of her fingers, checked her lipstick one more time, and hurried into the living room to the front door.

Dunne was dressed even less appropriately for the office than he had been the day before. His long, slim legs were encased in tight jeans. His broad shoulders were covered by soft plaid flannel. Under his arm he carried a blue nylon down jacket. Although his breath was visible in the morning air, he didn't seem to be cold.

He just stood on her porch, his hair shimmering in the slight breeze.

Maggie hesitated. Possibly, just possibly, she was about to do the wrong thing. Certainly Cass wouldn't approve of it.

Dunne gave her a slow, lazy smile. "Aren't you going to ask me in?" he chided. "It's cold out here, and I could use some coffee."

Maggie could have used some coffee herself, but there wasn't time. "We've got to get to Elm Street right away," she told him, not even bothering to say good morning. She gave him a swift summary of Clare Dobson's call. "I've got to get my coat," she told him. "Back in a minute."

She was gone less than half that time, but when she returned she found him still on the porch, frowning thoughtfully. For some reason the expression irritated her. What did he have to be pensive about? She'd been perfectly clear.

"If we don't hurry, Clare's going to have a nervous breakdown," she pointed out. "I told her I'd be right over. She'd already tried to call you. She's up there all by herself, and she sounded as if she were losing her mind."

Dunne didn't move. He gave her a puzzled glance, then turned to look up Mason Street. A small knot of public-school children, dressed in parkas and jeans, were waiting at the bus stop. Little clumps of plaid-uniformed parochial-school students were trailing south toward St. Stephen's Parish School. A young mother was loading an infant into an ancient Volkswagen. Dunne seemed inordinately interested in all of them.

"Hurry up," Maggie urged, beginning to feel nervousness settle in the pit of her stomach. "Clare's probably dead of apoplexy by now."

But Dunne still didn't move. He was staring up Mason Street, transfixed. "It's a nun," he said with a kind of boyish wonder. "A real nun. With a long dress and a veil and one of those wimple things. I didn't think they had those anymore."

Maggie sighed. Dunne had been very much distracted like this the night before, when he had first seen her house. He seemed to look on the neighborhood where she'd lived for all but four years of her life as something exotic and thoroughly charming.

"This is an Irish neighborhood," she snapped. "Of course there are nuns."

"It may be 'of course' to you," Dunne said, "but where I grew up, there wasn't even a neighborhood, never mind nuns."

"Where did you grow up?" Maggie asked, unable to stop herself. The last thing she wanted was to start a personal conversation with Dunne Holborn. She had plans for the man, and they didn't include feeling sorry for or intrigued by him. What was wrong with her, anyway?

But Dunne didn't seem interested in revealing personal information. He snapped out of his reverie and pulled on the down jacket, behaving as if he'd never heard her question.

"We'd better get going," he said, moving off the porch toward his car. "I was hoping I'd get a chance to talk things over with you privately, but it looks as if there won't be any time."

Maggie now had to hurry after him, irritated all over again. When *she* wanted to get moving, he just stood there. When *he* was ready to go, he expected her to drop everything and follow him. It was exactly the kind of behavior she had grown so used to in her ex-husband, and she hated it. Men like Ham and Dunne Holborn didn't really care what they did, as long as *they* were the ones who made the decision to do it.

She slid into the bucket seat on the passenger side of the Alfa Romeo and buckled her seat belt with an angry snap. "If you expect me to run off and do something, you ought to give me a little warning," she snapped.

Dunne ignored her annoyed tone. "Did you lock your door?" he asked solicitously.

"We don't lock our doors around here," Maggie retorted in exasperation. "If somebody tries to break into my house, Mrs. O'Shaughnessy will come after him with Timmy's baseball bat, and the intruder won't have a chance."

"My, my," Dunne clucked in what sounded like surprised but very real admiration. "It's remarkable. It's like a fairy tale."

"What it's like is an old ethnic neighborhood," Maggie said impatiently, "right down to the little old priest with an Irish accent, the old maid housekeeper with a mind like a CIA agent's, and a street full of people who know their neighbors' blood types. Sometimes that's wonderful, and sometimes it's enough to drive a sane woman to drink. Now, if you'll just get *moving . . .*"

"Yes, ma'am." In his painstakingly precise fashion, Dunne put the Alfa Romeo in gear and began to back it out of the driveway.

Finally they were getting started, Maggie thought.

But "finally" apparently hadn't come yet. Dunne slowed the car to a halt at the bottom of the drive, checked right and left for oncoming traffic, then let his gaze rest on her. This time there was no air of childlike awe about him. His green eyes were intent, almost like X rays in their searching, questioning glare.

Maggie began to feel the tingling in her skin and the roiling of her stomach. When Dunne looked at her like that, she felt almost naked. The worst part of that feeling was that, in a way, she liked it. Something hot and whipping like a flame blazed up her spine, and she had to fight to keep her eyes from closing and her lips from parting.

The cramped intimacy the car produced did nothing to mitigate her irrational but irresistible feelings. Dunne's muscular frame was hardly two inches away from her.

She could see every pore in the skin of his face, every vein in his strong hands. All she had to do was move a little to the left and she would be touching him.

He moved instead—not toward her but away. Maggie blinked in confusion. The change in his mood had been so swift, she hadn't even seen it happen. Now his eyes were half amused and half angry, and there was a stubborn twist to his mouth that she didn't like at all.

"I'll tell you what," he offered. "I'll warn you when I, as you put it, want you to run off and do something fast, and you'll be a good girl and tell me what you're up to."

Maggie flushed to the roots of her hair. "Why do you think I'm up to something?" she stammered. "I didn't make this up, if that's what you mean. Clare really did phone."

Dunne pursed his lips. "I'm sure she did," he said neutrally. "I don't doubt that at all." He stared at her for another long moment. Then, so suddenly that it made Maggie jump, he shifted forward and put the car in gear again.

"Here we go," he said, the challenge naked in his voice. "But let me tell you something, lady: If you're declaring war, I'm betting on me. I haven't lost one yet."

It was the worst drive Maggie had ever endured, and when they finally pulled into the company parking lot off Elm Street, she nearly fainted with relief. After all the trouble she'd had at Daystar, she hadn't thought she would ever be able to look on that 1930's pseudo-Gothic monstrosity with love, but now she did. Dunne had hardly pulled the car to a stop when she was leaping out of her seat, listening to the blessed sounds of her feet on the snow-wet pavement. Now, if they could just get inside and get started . . . ! Maybe once she had pulled that off she would be all right.

Certainly Dunne had done nothing on their drive to change her mind about the plan she'd made. He'd been silent, sullen, and superior, and if she hadn't been working overtime to keep her temper under control, she probably would have brained him. Besides, he'd made no attempt to correct the impression he'd left her with the previous night. The only reason she knew who he was, and what he was, was that Cass had told her.

A part of her brain warned that he just might have tried to explain, that she just might not have let him, but she brushed it away. Under the circumstances it was his responsibility to see that she knew what was going on.

At the renewed stirring of her anger she immediately felt better. When she indulged what she was convinced was her justified fury at the man, her head cleared and she was able to think. It was only when she allowed him to confuse her with that ingenuous quality of his or the gentlemanly airs he put on that she began to feel lost at sea.

She thought back on Cass's telephone call of the night before. Every time she thought of it—every time she realized what a fool Dunne Holborn had made of her— she wanted to spit.

He caught up to her just as she reached the elevators, and she couldn't prevent herself from treating him to a baleful glare.

"I'd ask what I've done," he said, "but I haven't been anywhere near you in the last sixty seconds. You sure you don't want to slow down and talk this out?"

"We've got a problem upstairs," Maggie said stiffly.

"That we do." The elevator door opened. "After you," he said gallantly.

Maggie scurried inside and pushed the button for the fourteenth floor. It was still early. The elevator was empty, and there was no sign of a secretary from the design department standing guard.

"Everything seems quiet enough so far," Dunne observed as the elevator stopped on fourteen.

Then the elevator doors opened, and the two of them were greeted with a scene that was anything but quiet. The tiny foyer and the narrow hallway leading off to the waiting room were crammed with people, every one of them dressed in a flowing blue robe with gold thread laced through it, every one of them wearing a tall, pointed hat, and every one of them carrying a wand. It was the wands that really got Maggie. Each of them was topped with a skull.

"Oh, no," she groaned, momentarily thrown off balance. "Do you think they're dangerous? I mean, those skulls . . ."

"Remember, all these people are devoted to science fiction," Dunne reminded her calmly. "You'll be fine. Just go up there, ask them what they want, and figure out a way to give it to them without destroying the game."

Maggie gave Dunne another baleful glance. Here he goes again, she thought furiously. She didn't care what Cass said; no matter who Dunne Holborn was, he was apparently addicted to letting other people do his dirty work. Well, he wasn't going to get away with it this time.

"Come with me," she hissed, grabbing him by the wrist. "I need you to back me up."

"Me?" he asked innocently. "I'm not the chief designer. I'm just a fifth wheel."

Maggie held on more tightly than before, her fury mounting. She started pushing through the crowd of sitting magicians, pulling him along behind her, intent on reaching the waiting-room door and the front of the crowd.

When she did, she shoved Dunne to the wall and turned to face the throng. Everybody seemed to be talking at once. Maggie took a deep breath and said, "Now!"

Almost instantly the talking stopped. Faces turned curiously in her direction. She was relieved to see that the people sitting closest to where she was standing seemed sane, even friendly. At least she wasn't going to have to calm an angry mob.

She cleared her throat and started in. "My name is Maggie Hennessy, and I'm chief designer of the L-Star game." There was a buzz at that, but it died down quickly.

"I'm not certain why you're here, but I guess it has something to do with the L-Star convention." There was a murmur of assent. "I'm sure that whatever it is you need, Daystar will be more than happy to accommodate you. We aim to please. Since you probably have a lot to talk about, let's get started."

She smiled at the crowd, then turned to Dunne. Grabbing his wrist again, she pulled him closer. "Just to make sure you're completely satisfied, I have brought with me Mr. Dunne Holborn, the originator of the total-environment game, the founder of Daystar, and the world's foremost expert on science fiction conventions."

Dunne's arm had gone rigid in her grasp. "What do you think you're doing?" he demanded angrily.

"Putting the ball in your court, Mr. Holborn," Maggie said through the smile she was still aiming at the assembled magicians. "Where it belongs."

"You may not like the way I'll play it," Dunne threatened.

"You wouldn't dare make a scene," Maggie taunted him. "You'd start a riot."

"Oh, I'll start a riot all right." He grabbed her shoulders and jerked her around to face him. "What I ought to do is spank you," he said. "But I think I'll do what I want to do instead."

Maggie didn't know what she had been expecting, but it wasn't what she got.

What she got was Dunne Holborn's hot, eager lips swooping down to capture her own.

Chapter Five

AT FIRST IT was wonderful. It was more wonderful than anything Maggie had ever known. Dunne's lips were slightly harsh and bittersweet, with a faint taste of hickory to them. For a moment that suggestion of hickory was all Maggie was aware of. Then the tip of his tongue began to slip tantalizingly along the roof of her mouth. Maggie felt the fire start at the base of her throat and begin to spread achingly over every inch of her skin. She moved instinctively toward him, leaning into his broad, sturdy frame. She felt the strong muscles of his arms as they held her to him, the bulging challenge of his thighs as they pressed against her own.

She had read about people being carried away by passion, but she had never believed in it. Now she was drowning in it, wanting the kiss to go on and on, wanting to feel the rough tips of Dunne's fingers promising, demanding, caressing. She kept her eyes closed and let the desire wash over her like a tidal wave. Surely this was the end of the universe. There was nothing better than this, nothing beyond this, nothing—

The sound of clapping penetrated Maggie's consciousness with the halting laziness of the last carbonation bubble floating to the surface of a glass of flat ginger ale. Somebody was applauding. But that was ridiculous. She and Dunne were alone.

Dunne began to move slowly backward, away from her. His lips released hers. For one suspended moment Maggie was aware of his face and nothing else. His mouth was curved in a soft smile. His eyes were wondering, gentle—at least she thought they were. Then she heard it again.

Somebody was clapping.

The shock was worse than being thrown into the Atlantic Ocean on the coldest day in February. The applause became louder, and there were a few whistles to go with it. Maggie turned slowly on her heel and looked out over the crowd of magicians. They were grinning, every last one of them. That incredibly private moment of passion had really been—what? An illusion? A hoax? A deliberate attempt to humiliate her?

The fire that spread through Maggie now had nothing to do with passion but a great deal to do with longing. She was furious, and she longed to let the great Dunne Holborn know it.

She turned to look at him. He was standing before the applauding crowd, bowing his head slightly, accepting his laurels. He thought he deserved a few congratulations, did he? Maggie fumed. Well, she'd show him. If he thought he could disarm her that way, then he was about to get a very nasty surprise.

She stepped up to him just as he was lifting his head from another mock bow. He looked amused, and that smirk on his face was going to make her job easier.

"Mr. Holborn," she commanded, her lips plastered with smiling determination, "I think what you just did deserves a prize. And here it is."

Then she slapped him resoundingly across the face.

Not until thirty seconds of total silence had passed did things start to happen. Maggie felt the grip of Dunne's fingers around her wrist at almost the same moment that he began to drag her toward the design-department door. She tried to wrench away from him.

"I'm not going in there," she warned him.

"Oh, yes you are," he announced, dragging her inexorably forward. "We need a little privacy."

"What for?" Maggie demanded with dripping sarcasm. "You didn't seem to feel a need for it a minute ago."

He answered her by kicking open the door and pulling her through it. Maggie made one last attempt to struggle, but it was useless. Dunne was too strong and too determined for her efforts to have any effect. Lifting her as if she were as weightless as a doll, he deposited her on the long beige Naugahyde visitors' couch and then turned to slam the door against the curious stares of the magicians outside.

"Do you want to tell me exactly what you think you're doing?" Maggie demanded, not deigning to rise from her seat.

"Paying you back in kind," Dunne responded with gleaming triumph. "You don't play fair, Margaret Mary Hennessy. And if you don't play fair, I don't see why I should."

"*I* don't play fair!" In spite of her determination to keep her cool and conduct this discussion in her most professional manner, Maggie found herself on her feet and moving. "You deliberately set out to make a fool of me. You started it last night. You let me do all that ranting and raving. You knew I didn't know who you were."

"I tried to tell you who I was," Dunne countered. "You wouldn't listen to me. You wouldn't listen to me even though I told you you were making a big mistake. We'll leave out the question of how you could possibly have filed a lawsuit against this company without knowing the name of the man who owns most of it. We'll chalk that up to an oversight, Ms. Hennessy. Let's keep this conversation on track. You're a pigheaded, stubborn, blind, willful—"

"Don't give me a list!" Maggie exploded. She paced over to Clare Dobson's desk and kicked one of its metal legs. Clare seemed to have disappeared, which was just as well. What Maggie was about to say was hardly for public consumption. She folded her arms across her chest and glared. "You listen to me, Mr. Holborn. I've been manipulated by experts. I've been pulled, pushed, folded, bent, and spindled, and it isn't going to happen again. After that little stunt you pulled in the hallway, it would serve you right if I filed sexual harassment charges to accompany the discrimination ones!"

"Stunt?" Dunne demanded, incredulous. "You call what I did a stunt?"

"What would you call it?"

"How about a little honesty for once? You're so defensive about being 'manipulated,' you see exploitation around every corner."

"You don't think making a fool of me in front of fifty people is exploiting me?" Maggie asked.

"How about admitting you want me as much as I want you?" Dunne suggested heatedly. "You go into sparks every time I come near you, and, if you don't know it, you're remarkably obtuse."

Maggie boiled. It wasn't enough that the man was an arrogant, high-handed, insufferable seven-letter word, he was an incredible egotist as well.

"Do me a favor," Maggie spat. "Take your arrogant hide and stuff it somewhere where I don't have to see it. I don't 'want you as much as you want me,' as you so originally put it. I don't want you, period. And let me tell you, I'm going to make damn sure I don't spend more than ten minutes alone in a room with you again."

"Are you really?" Dunne's green eyes glittered. He advanced on her, grinning with such triumphant glee that Maggie couldn't stop herself from stepping backward. Unfortunately, Clare's desk was right behind her. The back of her legs bumped against it, and she came to a halt. She was trapped.

Dunne pressed close to her, towering nearly a foot above her head and making her shiver. "If you wish to quit your job, Ms. Hennessy, I'll expect your resignation on my desk at four o'clock today."

"I've got absolutely no intention of quitting my job," Maggie said angrily. "And if you try to fire me after that attack you made on me, I'll go to court and get an injunction to stop you."

"Will you, now? Well, then, we're going to have to spend more than ten minutes alone in a room together again, and soon. We have a project to finish, a convention to attend, and a game to run. We're going to spend four days living in each other's laps—unless, of course, you want to blow both your case and your job by leaving now."

Maggie took a deep, painful, exasperated breath. And she thought she'd been manipulated by experts! This man was Machiavelli. Any way she turned, she was cornered.

She closed her eyes, willing away her intense desire to haul off and slug him. She had to think, and she certainly wasn't going to be able to think with Dunne standing only inches away from her. She had to talk to Cass. The situation was completely impossible. There had to be a way out.

She opened her eyes again and began to sidle away from him, inching her way to freedom. When she'd made her way to the back door that led to the inner corridors, she turned and told Dunne, "There are a lot of magicians out there. They're counting on you."

Then she whirled away from him and made her escape.

Cass's office was in a gargoyled monstrosity on Church Street, four blocks from the similar building that housed the Daystar design offices. Maggie splashed through her fourth consecutive puddle and ducked into the overly ornate lobby, shaking the rain from her hair. November was often a rainy or snowy season in New Haven, but this was insane. She hadn't been able to stay dry for days.

She punched the button for the elevator and jumped a little when the door opened almost immediately. It was the only elevator in the building, and it usually took a good twenty minutes to summon it. Maggie looked nervously around the empty foyer. What time was it, anyway? If it was too early, Cass might not even be in her office yet.

She punched the button for the fourth floor and stood at the back of the car while the door creaked closed. The idea that she might not find Cass was unnerving. Maggie's anger had cooled considerably on the way over. What was left was the fear and the wound-to-the-breaking-point tension she felt whenever she thought of her present predicament. Too much was hanging in the balance. Her job, her future, her very life depended on the outcome of a case she seemed perversely determined to sabotage at every possible opportunity. Add to that her conflicting reactions to Dunne Holborn, and you had the stuff of a disaster movie.

Maybe Cass had been right. Maybe she should have filed a class-action suit instead of an individual suit. Maggie shook her head. A class-action suit forced a company to hire women—any women—in numbers determined by the court. Only an individual suit gave her the opportunity to prove that she was good at her job and not just another neglected member of a minority group.

The elevator opened on four and she stepped out, turning automatically to the right. If Cass wasn't in already, she'd just camp on her doorstep until she got in. She needed some advice, some sympathy, and some good common sense before she'd be ready to return to that snake pit.

"It's locked," Cass said from behind her. "What are you doing here at eight-thirty in the morning?"

Maggie jumped. "Where did you come from?" she demanded. "There wasn't anyone else in the elevator."

"I was in the ladies' room." Cass nodded in the direction of a cul-de-sac at the end of the hall. "So what gives?"

"I've got a little problem," Maggie confessed.

"Another one?" Cass moaned. "The business day hasn't even started yet."

Cass's office was a large, high-ceilinged square full of furniture that should have been given a decent burial in 1926. Maggie took a seat in an overstuffed monster upholstered in faded red plush, kicked off her shoes, and tucked her feet under her.

"Sit down," she told Cass. "It may help."

Half an hour later Maggie was exhausted and Cass had pulled enough hairs from her head to make a small red wig, but the story had been told.

"I was thinking all the way over here that maybe I ought to quit." Maggie sighed. "I'm probably doing more damage this way than I would if I just walked out."

Cass shook her head vigorously. "What would you do if you quit?" she demanded. "You don't have another job waiting for you, and you won't get one if people find out you're suing Daystar. Holborn could use the fact that no one else is hiring you against you."

Maggie started to say he wouldn't do a thing like that. Then she stopped. As far as she knew, Dunne Holborn would do anything to get his own way. She shook her head, a little disturbed by her momentary aberration. "It would be his word against mine," she told Cass. "You said yourself that the judges in this state tend to give more weight to the woman's testimony."

"Usually they do," Cass nodded. "In this case we've got a little problem. I spent half the night and most of the morning doing research on Dunne Holborn. Want to hear what I've got?"

"Do I have to?" Maggie groaned.

Cass pulled a manila folder toward her and opened it. "Bachelor of science from Yale," she recited, "summa cum laude. In physics, no less. Phi Beta Kappa. Master of science in artificial intelligence—computer design, to you—from MIT. Graduated second in the class, which consisted of approximately five hundred people. Produced the first total-environment game, called Options, to teach high school students what their futures would be like if they took various scholastic and training programs. He was at MIT at the time. By the time he picked up that master's degree, he was selling Options to over two thousand school districts nationwide. He started Daystar when he graduated, at the age of twenty-five—"

"That's enough," Maggie interrupted. "It doesn't mean he isn't a sexist, and it doesn't mean he isn't discriminating against women."

"No," Cass admitted, "but it does mean he's an expert. And you've got the job you want, Maggie. You just want a chance to do it and prove you can do it well. Dunne Holborn is the world's foremost expert on what you do."

"Don't tell me," Maggie said with growing agitation. "I don't just have to get along with the man; I have to convince him I'm his most talented employee."

"It wouldn't hurt," Cass said wryly.

"It also won't work."

Cass sighed. "Somehow I agree with you," she said. "Unfortunately it doesn't change my advice. You want to hear it?"

"Go ahead," Maggie said glumly.

"You can't quit," Cass said bluntly. "You've got to

go back to work, do what you have to do to get your job done right, and fend off Mr. Holborn as best you can. Or as best you want to."

"Don't start that again," Maggie said nervously.

"I won't," Cass promised. "But believe me, you can't quit. Daystar will destroy us in court if you do. I'm not kidding when I say you'll never work again."

Maggie unfolded her legs and plunged her feet into her wet shoes.

"Why is it," she asked Cass, "that I only seem to hear bad news these days?"

"Tut, tut," Cass chided. "You wouldn't want to hear only good news. You'd be bored to tears."

Maggie threw herself across Cass's desk in mock desperation. "Bore me!" she pleaded. "Bore me!"

"Mr. Holborn's office called," Clare Dobson said when Maggie, soaking wet again, finally straggled into the design department. "Five times."

"Was he threatening execution or something a little more elaborate?" Maggie asked, taking the message slips.

"He said he wanted to deliver the specifications for the, uh, Pterotopeths." Clare glanced nervously at the door. "He finally sent a messenger. I had them put everything they could on your desk."

"The Pterotopeths went home, I take it," Maggie said absently, fingering the pile of notes. "Did we get any messages from friendly aliens, or just these bulletins from the war zone?"

"A Sister Joan Marie called," Clare said. "She wants to know if you can pick up some books at St. Raphael's Rectory tonight and bring them over to the convent at St. Stephen's when you come." Clare fiddled with her glasses. "Are you joining a convent, Miss Hennessy?"

"No," Maggie said with a grin, "although I'm beginning to think it wouldn't be such a bad idea." Seeing that Clare still looked puzzled, she explained, "Sister Joan Marie and her nuns are giving an Advent party for the elderly in my neighborhood. I promised to help out."

Clare nodded, satisfied. "Then there's this," she said. She reached to the floor and came up with one of the magician's skull-headed wands. "A member of the Pterotopeths sent you this." She handed the wand to Maggie. "It's supposed to be good for getting a man to do what you want him to do. Or so she said."

Maggie hefted the heavy wand. Up close it didn't look so frightening; the skull was obviously plastic. "Well," she told Clare, "if the magic doesn't work, I can always brain him with it. It weighs a ton." She tucked the wand under her arm. "I'm going to go work on those specifications. If Cass calls, put her through. If it's anybody else, tell him I'm out, gone, disappeared, taking up residence on Mars. I don't care."

"Even Mr. Holborn?"

"Especially Mr. Holborn," Maggie said firmly.

Clare gave her a quick, perplexing, wicked little grin but made no further comment.

Maggie hurried down the corridor to her office. Everybody seemed to be going crazy at once. If she could just find five minutes of peace, she might be able to get something done.

She reached the door of her office, turned the knob, and pushed the door open with her foot. Five minutes of peace and quiet, she told herself. That's all I ask. That's all I really want. That's—

She stopped. She breathed deeply. She backed up.

Impossible. It was categorically impossible.

She took another step forward and peered into her office. Impossible it might be, but apparently it was real.

The whole room was awash with flowers. Roses, violets, gentians, gladiolus, carnations, tulips, irises, lilacs, geraniums, orchids, gardenias, and lilies of the valley covered every available surface. Some were even hanging from hooks in the ceiling.

Maggie leaned weakly against the door frame. Some-

where, she knew, there was going to be a card with
Dunne Holborn's name on it.

She rubbed her eyes. She was going to have a headache.

She was going to have a flying migraine.

Chapter Six

MAGGIE WASN'T SURPRISED to find Dunne Holborn's sleek Alfa Romeo parked in front of her house when she got home from work. She just pulled around it into the driveway, parked beside Ted O'Shaughnessy's battered station wagon, and shut off her ignition. Of course Dunne was there, waiting for her. Where else would he be? The man obviously never went home.

Maggie took a minute to consider her reaction to the situation. Was she glad or sorry that Dunne seemed to be pursuing her? Did she want him to disappear or continue? She didn't have any answers.

She climbed out of the car. She knew what Cass would say. Cass would sarcastically ask: What did she want, a lawsuit or a love affair? Naturally, Cass would order her to pick the lawsuit.

Dunne was sitting on the green metal glider on her

side of the front porch, his hands laced behind his head, his feet propped on the porch railing, an open book in his lap. The book was a historical novel by Roberta Gellis. Maggie smiled slightly. In some strange way it fit him.

Dunne got to his feet. Maggie watched the uncoiling of his strong, lean body with something like awe. No matter how angry she got at the man, he never failed to set off that tingling in her spine.

She shook off the feeling and walked past him to the door. "I don't know what you're doing here," she said as ominously as she could manage, "but don't you think you've done enough for one day?"

Dunne grinned. "Did you like my apology?" he asked. "I thought it was the perfect gesture."

"So did the Daystar software division in Anaheim, California," Maggie retorted. "They're waiting for the second installment."

"Anaheim?" Dunne looked puzzled. "What's Anaheim got to do with it?"

"Clare Dobson called a friend of hers out there who's secretary to your operating vice-president for software." Maggie fitted her key into the lock. "She also called her married sister in Tucson and her cousin Angela in Sault Sainte Marie, Michigan. We're on a national hookup."

Dunne seemed to consider that for a moment. Then he grinned, his green eyes sparkling. "Well, then," he said, sounding absurdly self-satisfied, "I take it I'm forgiven."

Maggie kicked the front door open, not knowing if she was furious or just exasperated. She hated willful, domineering men, and Dunne certainly was one of those, even if he did go about it in a more pleasant way than Hamlin had. Dunne always disarmed her, period.

She stomped into the house. "I called Cass about your little stunt with the flowers," she warned Dunne.

"Cass?" he queried.

"My lawyer, Cass Delaney," she said threateningly.

"As far as she's concerned, it was a deliberate attempt to discredit me."

Dunne paused in the doorway, frowning. "Is that what *you* think it was?" he asked, his voice serious.

"Let's just say that if it wasn't, then you're much less intelligent than I thought you were. How do you think something like that looks?"

Dunne followed her in and dropped onto the couch, his face grave. "You're right," he said. "I didn't think of that. I suppose it's because—"

"Because what?" Maggie asked suspiciously.

"Nothing." Dunne's face cleared. A moment before he had been serious and concerned; now he was blandly inquiring. "Why don't I buy you another dinner?" he suggested. "My choice of restaurants this time. That way I'll have a chance to apologize for apologizing in such a thoughtless manner, explain my behavior of this morning, and iron out our differences. You owe me at least that much," he added, pointedly rubbing the cheek she'd slapped.

Maggie threw her hands into the air. "I don't owe you anything," she told him, "except good work, and I'd give you that if you'd let me. Why don't you just go home?"

"I don't want to go home," Dunne said. "I like it here."

"Fine," Maggie said shortly. "Watch it for me while I'm out, will you? I'm going to be late."

"Late for what?" Dunne looked thunderously suspicious, and Maggie felt her stomach jump. She shouldn't let herself be so affected by his every mood, she told herself. He was just being a spoiled child, angry because he couldn't get what he wanted this time. Well, he might not like it, but he was just going to have to lump it.

"It's nothing you'd be interested in," she told him coolly. "I've got to serve pastry and sing carols over at St. Stephen's. They're having an Advent party for the Senior Citizens Club."

Dunne brightened immediately. "Wonderful. I'll go with you."

Maggie stared at him, appalled. "You can't go with me. You'd be bored silly. It isn't your kind of place. It's a lot of little old ladies!"

"I love little old ladies," Dunne said firmly. "And they love me back. Let's go."

"It's not just that you don't take no for an answer," Maggie fumed, "you don't even bother to ask the question. What if I don't want you to go with me?"

"Won't make any difference at all," Dunne conceded.

"Does it ever occur to you to consider what other people want once in a while?" Maggie flared. "Does it ever occur to you to put someone else's needs above your own?"

"Sometimes. But not right now. Right now you're being unreasonable."

"*I'm* being unreasonable?" Maggie exclaimed. "You walk in here and take over my life, and then you've got the nerve to tell me I'm being unreasonable?"

"Who's driving?" Dunne asked. "You or me?"

"Nobody's driving!" Maggie erupted.

"Good." Dunne grinned. "Walking distance. Perfect."

By the time Maggie had changed into jeans and a soft, midnight-blue angora sweater, brushed her teeth and hair, and retrieved from her car the songbooks she had picked up at St. Raphael's, it was snowing again. Dunne stood beside her in the driveway, his scarf wound around his neck, his hat pulled down around his ears, and his hands in his pockets. Maggie gave him the songbooks to carry and marched out to Mason Street.

Bundled up the way he was, Dunne looked almost like a little boy whose mother had wrapped him into immobility in his snowsuit. He was somehow endearing that way, and Maggie didn't want to look at him while he was being endearing. She wanted to stay mad at him.

She had every right to stay mad at him. He had the most annoying habit of taking it for granted that she was going to do anything he wanted her to, when he wanted her to.

He trudged up to her through the snow. "These things look a hundred years old." He hefted the ancient brown-covered songbooks in his hands. "I think the bindings are unraveling."

"You should see the ones at St. Stephen's," Maggie told him, beginning to lead him south toward Ellery Street. "These are in pristine condition compared to those. That's why I had to pick them up."

"Why don't they just buy new ones?" Dunne asked.

Maggie shrugged. Explaining life on Mason Street to someone with a background like Dunne Holborn's would probably be impossible. "Songbooks are expensive," she pointed out, "and they're not a necessity. The people around here aren't poor, but they've all got large families to support. If they don't have children, they've got aging parents and sometimes even grandparents. They give what they can to the parish, but it isn't always a lot of money. So . . ."

"So," Dunne mused. He scratched his chin. "I take it there *are* necessities, then? Things to spend money on instead of songbooks?"

"Of course there are," Maggie told him. "There's a day-care program for working mothers—a lot of mothers in this neighborhood work; there's a program where invalids and old people are brought a hot meal every day; sometimes the nuns go out and clean house for people who can't do it for themselves; and there's the school."

Dunne whistled. "Haven't you people ever heard of the welfare state?" he asked.

"We do for ourselves out here," Maggie said sharply. "We don't need the government dole." Then she blushed furiously. "I'm sorry," she apologized. "That was a perfect imitation of my grandmother Foley. I didn't mean to sound so self-righteous."

"You sound fine." He reached out with his free hand and brushed her hair with his fingers. The touch made Maggie feel hot even in the cold wind of the street, but she didn't move away. When she made herself stop thinking about all the possible dire consequences of her being attracted to this man, she liked the heat he made her feel.

"The only thing I don't understand," Dunne said, "is what you're doing here. I've looked through your records, you know. You make a very decent salary. You could afford a condominium in Orange if you wanted it, or an apartment in New Haven in one of the new complexes. Why here?"

"I grew up here," Maggie said tightly, feeling her throat constrict. "Besides, I lived in a complex once," she continued. "It was a housing complex in California. I didn't like it."

"No? Somehow I'm not surprised. I can't see you in California."

Maggie grimaced. "I can't, either. When I look back on it, I think I must have been nuts. At the time, though, it seemed to make a lot of sense."

"At the time?"

Maggie sighed. "I was seventeen years old and had recently graduated from high school. I didn't want to go to college, and I didn't want to find a job in New Haven and live at home like a good little Irish girl. I wanted wanted to see LIFE in capital letters."

"And you thought California was the place to do that?" Dunne didn't wait for an answer. "But you have a college degree," he said. "I saw that on your record. And it's local."

"Albertus Magnus," Maggie agreed. "That was after I came back."

They had reached the door of St. Stephen's, and Maggie stopped, reaching out to take the songbooks from Dunne. She really didn't want to continue this conversation. The time she thought of as "the California episode" was embarrassing even to think of, and what had happened between her and Hamlin Marshall was still too close to her heart. She wasn't ready to share that with Dunne yet.

There was a creaking at the top of the stairs, and light streamed from the open church door. Sister Joan Marie, a vigorous-looking middle-aged woman in a knee-length gray habit and short black veil, stood on the top step, peering down at them. Maggie sighed with relief. Saved by the bell—this time, at least.

"Maggie!" the nun trumpeted, then paused. "Who's that you've got with you?"

"This is my boss, Mr. Dunne Holborn. I don't know if he's English or an Orangeman, but one way or another he's inimical to the cause."

"I'm a Scot, Sister," Dunne said as he glided into the foyer of the parish center, "and I'm not inimical to anything but stale cigarette smoke."

"Stay away from Mr. Clancy, then," Sister Joan Marie said. "He's been smoking the same cigar since 1924."

Maggie took the songbooks and marched into the main hall, a little disturbed at the ease with which Dunne was making friends with Sister Joan Marie. This was Maggie's world. It was bad enough that Dunne had to barge into it and start giving orders. He ought to have the grace not to fit in so easily.

She put the songbooks on a table and turned to survey the room. Mr. Clancy was sitting by himself in one corner. About two dozen little old ladies were sitting in a clump in another corner. Every last one of them was staring straight at Dunne.

Maggie groaned.

"Look over there," Dunne said, coming up behind her and whispering in her ear. "The one fiddling with the teacups. I think she's looking at you."

Maggie took a quick glance at Sister Hyacinth, her body draped in a long gray robe, her hair and half her forehead covered in white, a black veil hanging down her back and past her waist.

"She's staring at *you*," Maggie told Dunne. "And why not? So is everyone else."

"Why don't you introduce me to her." Dunne cupped her elbow in his hand. "I wouldn't want to do the wrong thing."

"You couldn't do the wrong thing if you burned the place down," Maggie said sourly. "They adopted you the minute you walked into the room."

"Now, now," Dunne said lightly. "Mustn't be jealous."

"I'm not jealous!" Maggie exploded.

"Protective," Dunne amended. "You're protecting your turf." Seeing Maggie blush, he grinned. "I won't take it over on you, I promise."

"I'm not worried about your taking it over on me," Maggie said, but Dunne's analysis was too close to the truth for comfort, and her statement lacked force.

She looked up to see Sister Hyacinth peering eagerly at Dunne through her thick wire-rimmed lenses. Then the nun turned and stared at Maggie with a cold, glinting, all-remembering eye.

"Fifth grade," Sister Hyacinth said. "Same year as Caroline Delaney. Always passing notes."

This time Maggie's blush reached the roots of her hair, and it didn't help that Dunne was so obviously striving not to laugh. It was all she could do to keep from drowning the woman in her own teapot and then going to work on the grinning man beside her.

"This is Dunne Holborn, Sister," Maggie said, trying to regain her dignity. "He's—"

She never had a chance to finish. Sister Hyacinth was beaming at Dunne.

"You look like a hungry man, Mr. Holborn," the nun said cheerfully.

"Exactly what I was thinking, Sister," Mrs. Gilligan crowed, making her slow way toward the tea table. She reached up and patted one of Dunne's muscular arms. "He doesn't eat right at all, I don't think."

"Mrs. Gilligan made tea cookies," Sister Hyacinth said archly.

"Wonderful," Dunne promptly responded.

Maggie turned away in disgust. Maybe if she worked very hard at it, she would find a way *not* to spend the evening watching the great Mr. Dunne Holborn being the life of this particular party.

"Getting ready to go?" Sister Joan Marie asked, gliding up to Maggie as the latter stuffed her thick black hair under her woolen hat.

"If I can tear the rock star over there away from his teeming fans." Maggie gave a toss of her head in the direction of the corner. Then she grinned. She'd been telling herself for the past two hours that she shouldn't be jealous of Dunne's instant popularity. The old people who frequented St. Stephen's Parish House had little enough to amuse them, and if seeing a big, good-looking young man like Dunne Holborn eat his way to obesity made them happy, she should be glad of it. "How much did he eat, anyway?" she asked Sister Joan Marie.

The nun smiled. "One of everything," she said, amused. "He even managed to get down one of Martha Fitzgibbon's rum balls. For that he may very well be canonized."

"Let's just hope he doesn't get sick."

Sister Joan Marie shook her head. "I do have to thank you for bringing him," she said. "It was one of the better ideas anyone's had around here in I don't know how long. They'll remember this party for years."

"Sister Hyacinth asked him to come back next year," Maggie said, thinking of the trouble she'd taken to pick up the songbooks and the hours she had spent helping to clean the main room the weekend before. Those had been her real contributions to the party. It was a little disconcerting to realize she'd done all that work and nobody seemed to remember it. All they could think about was Dunne Holborn.

Maggie was about to give him a sour look, when the sight of him bending solicitously over old Mrs. O'Brien's wheelchair made her soften. She had to say this much for Dunne Holborn: He didn't reserve his charm for people who could get him somewhere. He was capable of being caring and concerned about people he didn't even know.

He patted Mrs. O'Brien's shoulder one last time and started toward Maggie. "What's the matter?" he asked.

"I'm just tired," Maggie mumbled, feeling embarrassed and a little awkward.

"We'll just have to get you home to bed," Dunne said wickedly.

Maggie nearly jumped out of her skin. "Nuns," she hissed. *"Nuns."*

"Lots of nuns," Dunne admitted cheerfully. He came closer, and Maggie instinctively backed up. It wasn't until she saw the coats hanging on hooks all around her that she realized he had gradually backed her into the tiny cloakroom just beyond the front door of the parish center. She heard the click of the door closing and looked around frantically, trying to force her eyes to adjust to the darkness. For the moment they were as alone as they would be on a desert island—except for the large potential audience standing just outside the door.

Dunne leaned over her, pressing his palms against the wall behind her and trapping her with his strong arms. Maggie couldn't stop the heat from rising within her. Even the knowledge that her fifth-grade teacher was standing only a few feet away didn't break the sudden swelling tide of her desire. If anything, it oddly intensified her response to Dunne. There was something faintly exciting about being only moments away from discovery.

"Well, well," Dunne murmured, stepping closer to her.

"Do these things just sort of come on you, like fits?" Maggie gasped. "Two minutes ago you weren't even thinking of—of this kind of thing."

"I'm always thinking of this kind of thing," Dunne quipped. "Besides"—he looked upward—"two minutes ago I wasn't standing under mistletoe."

Maggie followed the direction of Dunne's gaze. It was there, all right, hanging less than an inch from his soft brown hair.

"Why do I have this feeling you put it there yourself?" Maggie asked dryly.

Dunne grinned. "Because I did. I moved it from the doorway of the meeting room."

"Dunne," Maggie warned, "this isn't the time or place for this."

"Nonsense." Dunne leaned closer, so close that his lips brushed her ear. "That's what mistletoe is for," he whispered. "Besides, look at all the trouble I went to to get you a little privacy this time."

"It's not going to be so private if someone decides to come in and get a coat," Maggie said desperately.

"Then we'll have to act fast," Dunne teased. "Every minute we waste brings us another minute closer to discovery."

Maggie's emotions were so confused, she knew she'd never be able to sort them out. She wanted to kiss Dunne, grab her coat, and run, all at the same time. Her saner instincts told her to do the latter, but when she looked around for a way out, she realized there wasn't one. Dunne had her backed into a corner. He was leaning over her, tall and broad and strong, inclining his head for her kiss.

Maggie felt a sudden surge of resolve. Obviously there was only one thing to do, and if she had any sense, she'd do it quickly. She had no idea what had prompted this insane stunt of his, but she knew what she was going to do about it.

She fixed him with a mock baleful glare. Then she jumped up and threw her arms around his neck.

Chapter Seven

MAGGIE HAD IT all planned. Her kiss was going to be swift, savage, and surprising. Instead of the lingering embrace he was expecting, Dunne would get nothing more than a quick peck beside his lips. There wouldn't be time for anyone to come in and discover them. It would all be over before he knew it. Then she would take her coat and walk calmly into the foyer.

It didn't work out that way. Maggie didn't know if it was her unconquerable attraction to the man or Dunne's own expertise, but hardly had she felt the lightly haired nape of his neck against her palms than she began to melt. Dunne's lips were rough and cool and softly inviting. They pressed against hers with infinite gentleness, caressing, coaxing. There was no naked sexual challenge. The warm honey that spread through every nerve

in her body made her think of long winter nights before
a fire and lazy Sunday-morning breakfasts in bed under
thick goose-down quilts. Long love, lasting love, Maggie
thought, her body seeming to flow effortlessly toward
Dunne's broad chest.

Dunne's kiss seemed to heighten all her senses, bringing the world closer rather than shutting it out. She thought
she knew the position of every coat on every peg in the
cloakroom. She was hypersensitively aware of every person in the meeting room and the foyer—the nuns, the
old people who had known her since she was first born.
She felt gloriously alive and much more susceptible to
Dunne's embrace than she would have expected.

She felt his arms sliding up her back as an electric
flood that started at the base of her spine and traveled,
pulsing, upward. Her skin began to warm. Her breasts
felt large against the lacy binding of her bra under her
sweater. The long winter nights and breakfasts in bed
were still there, but now they held a spicy undercurrent.
Maggie wanted to know all the secrets Dunne's body
seemed to promise her, and she wanted to know them
right away. She pressed her lips against his, wishing there
were a way to lock the cloakroom door and stay se-
questered with Dunne for half a century.

She felt him ease away and, awkward and confused,
stepped back herself. Her nerve endings refused to dull
to their everyday level of awareness. Even in the darkness
of the cloakroom, objects seemed clearer, colors brighter,
than Maggie could remember them.

"I thought you were worried about being caught,"
Dunne teased. "We must have been in here fifteen minutes."

Maggie was stunned. What had she done? She had to
be crazy! She hadn't even wanted to kiss Dunne Holborn.
Or had she? Dunne had moved away and was rummaging
among the coats for theirs. Maggie gave him a long,
curious look. The truth of the matter was that she had
certainly wanted to kiss Dunne Holborn while she was

kissing him, and she couldn't blame it on being carried away by passion, either. She'd been wide awake the whole time, and she'd loved every minute of it.

The whole idea made her distinctly uneasy. She knew men like Dunne Holborn. She knew herself, too. With a man like Dunne she would have to fight or be crushed. There was no place in such a situation for any kind of meaningful human relationship. The only thing she'd get for giving in to her attraction to this man was hurt.

Dunne came up behind her, their coats folded over his arm. "Are you ready to leave?" he prodded. "Or are you supposed to stay to clean up?"

"No, no," Maggie said hurriedly. "We can leave whenever we want. I ought to get home and go to bed, anyway."

Dunne leaned over and pushed the door open. The light was momentarily blinding, but Maggie's vision adjusted rapidly—almost too rapidly, she thought with half-amused dismay. She wasn't so sure she wanted to know that the entire population of the Advent party was sitting outside the cloakroom door, patiently waiting for them to emerge.

"Isn't that nice," Mrs. Fitzgibbon gushed. "I always think that's nice, two young people in love."

"That's what you call love?" Mrs. Gilligan snorted. "We did a lot better at love in my day."

"Well, it isn't your day," Mrs. Fitzgibbon retorted. "Leave the children alone."

Maggie had to stop herself from laughing out loud. The beaming circle of nuns and old people looked so pleased. They'd all known her forever, and now they thought they had the rest of her life mapped out for her. She didn't think she'd tell any of them just how tentative her relationship with Dunne Holborn really was.

She tugged impatiently on Dunne's sleeve. "Let's go," she whispered.

Dunne grinned his wicked grin. "You say you want to go home?" His voice was loud enough to be heard in

New Jersey. "I suppose the party *is* over."

Maggie was ready to kick him. "You don't have to live here," she muttered, getting a little nervous. She already knew Dunne well enough to realize that once he got started, he didn't know when to stop. And she didn't think she wanted to find out how far he'd take his little joke. "Home," she ordered him quietly. "Get moving."

"Well," Dunne announced loudly, "if you have to get up early, I guess we ought to get you home to bed."

Maggie caught the gleam in Sister Hyacinth's eyes and nearly groaned aloud. This time Maggie did kick him in the ankle. He didn't even wince. She grabbed his arm and started dragging him toward the door.

"I've got an early day tomorrow, Sister." Maggie reached out and gave Sister Joan Marie's hand a quick shake. "Good evening, Mrs. Gilligan. I hope your arthritis gets better. Good evening, Sister." Maggie didn't dare look Sister Hyacinth in the face. She plunged out the door of the parish center and started tramping through the light snow.

Dunne stopped a moment at the door to say a few final words, but Maggie didn't wait for him. She slogged along, the cold wind making her burning ears feel like the live wires of an electrical heater. Of all the fool things to have done! She ought to be ready to murder Dunne for pulling that little prank.

Instead she felt like laughing. It wouldn't take those old ladies half an hour to spread the story around the parish, and she'd be hearing about it for the next forty years!

She heard footsteps pounding heavily behind her and turned to face Dunne before he had a chance to reach her.

"What did you think you were doing?" she demanded, suppressing a laugh. "I thought you were trying to embarrass me professionally, not personally. I'm never going to live that down."

Dunne gave her a long, quizzical look. "You're not

mad at me?" he asked tentatively.

Maggie shook her head. "I ought to be," she told him. "I ought to be ready to behead you. Unfortunately the whole thing was too funny, and I did manage to get us out of there in time. But what did you think you were doing?"

Dunne coughed, then looked into her face and smiled. He rocked back and forth on his heels. What he didn't do was answer her.

"Are you just going to stand there until I pick a topic of conversation you find more congenial?" Maggie asked in exasperation.

Dunne grabbed her arm and started walking toward Noble Street, the length of his stride and the strength of his grip forcing her along. "Let's talk about our future," he said pleasantly.

"I don't want to talk about our future," Maggie said, trying not to stumble. "Do you always have to pick every topic of conversation?"

"I don't pick every topic of conversation."

"Mr. Holborn, you not only pick every topic of conversation, you want to be the one to determine everything else, too. Which car I ride to work in in the morning. When we fight. When we kiss . . ."

"You did a pretty good job of picking when we'd fight this morning," Dunne pointed out.

"Which you turned into an occasion when we kissed," Maggie answered. "And you've never once bothered to inquire whether I even wanted to kiss you."

Dunne stopped dead in his tracks, the sudden movement making Maggie pitch forward and nearly fall.

"But you do want to kiss me," he said seriously. "You want more than that, too. I can tell. That's why I wanted to talk about our future."

Maggie sighed. She couldn't very well say she didn't want him to touch her. Her response to him was too powerful to be hidden, even from herself.

"Maybe it would help if you tried asking me some-

times," she explained. "You just leap at me and tell me
what to do. Sometimes you don't even bother to tell me.
You make up your mind, grab me by the arm, and expect
me to go along." Maggie peered around at the quiet
streets that surrounded them. It was only eleven o'clock,
but most of the houses were already dark. "Take right
now," Maggie suggested. "Just where are we going?"

Dunne looked surprised. "I'm taking you home," he
said. "That's what you wanted to do, isn't it?"

Maggie shook her head. "You're lost, Mr. Holborn.
If we walked long enough in this direction, we might
get to New Haven, but we'd never get to Mason Street."

"Of course we would," Dunne insisted. "I was watching very carefully when we left your house."

Maggie threw up her hands. "Don't you see what I
mean? This is *my* neighborhood. I've lived here most of
my life. You're here for two hours, and already you
know more about it than I do—or you think you do! It
doesn't matter what or who or when, you've got to control it. It makes me feel pushed around, Dunne. And I
won't stand for it."

Dunne scratched his chin thoughtfully. His green eyes
were dark and serious in his strongly angled face, and
the cold wind was whipping through his hair.

Suddenly Maggie longed to brush the hair out of his
face. He'd been kind and considerate to the old people
that night, and respectful to the nuns. That was behavior
she could admire in anyone. Under Dunne's forceful,
domineering facade, there was a man Maggie was beginning to think she could . . . respect.

She found herself staring into his eyes and backed
away a little. What did she think she was doing? Why
did she have to oversimplify things like that? Dunne
might not be a phony like Ham, but Maggie knew herself
well enough to realize that she could never find much
happiness with a man who always wanted to be boss.
She'd start feeling resentful and end up feeling suffo-
cated. She needed breathing room, a chance to grow and

excel as her own person. And Dunne Holborn would never give her that. He wasn't capable of giving it to anyone. And she couldn't go back to being a dutiful little woman—not after Ham.

Besides, there was the lawsuit. For all she knew, Dunne was playing up to her in the hope that she would drop her suit and save the company a lot of money and trouble. For some reason she wasn't really able to believe that anymore, but she knew she shouldn't rule it out. Cass would kill her.

"I think I've got it worked out," Dunne's voice boomed through the darkness.

"Got what worked out?" Maggie asked curiously, her thoughts still muddled.

"You think I order you around too much," Dunne said slowly. "That's the basic problem, not the lawsuit."

"The lawsuit's important," Maggie said quickly, thinking of Cass with a guilty pang.

"The lawsuit can take care of itself," Dunne replied, dismissing it. "The real problem is that you think I treat you like a—like a—"

"I think *sex object* would be going too far," Maggie said dryly.

Dunne grinned his acquiescence. "It's not for lack of trying," he quipped. Then he grew serious again. "All right, Maggie, you say I push you around. I'm not going to deny it. I've been accused of it before, and I'm probably guilty. But you're not that easy to deal with yourself, you know. I never know when you're going to fly off the handle."

Maggie bit her lip. She didn't really have an answer to Dunne's charge. It was true enough. She could hardly tell him that "flying off the handle" was the only way she felt she could deal with him when he got into one of his bossy moods. *She* might know that her only choices seemed to be an outburst or docility, but it probably wouldn't make any sense to him.

"There's one more thing," Dunne said. "You *could*

admit you were at least half to blame this morning. You did goad me into that 'stunt.'"

Maggie relaxed. This was something she could handle.

"You never gave me a chance," she said. "I was ready to apologize after I calmed down. The flowers got to me first. Then you showed up at my door."

"Apologize now," Dunne teased, seemingly content to slide into her bantering mood. He stepped in front of her and drew himself up against her. "I can think of hundreds of ways for you to make it up to me."

Maggie stepped around him quickly, remembering the cloakroom and not ready to repeat her surrender. "How about if we do something at *my* suggestion for a change," she said lightly. "Something you haven't tried before."

Dunne's eyebrows shot up comically. "Something I haven't tried before? How do you know there is such a thing?"

Maggie grinned. "I know you've never been in this neighborhood before," she said, "at least not until this morning. Ergo—"

"Ergo what?"

"You've never climbed this particular tree."

Maggie was gratified to see Dunne look distinctly nonplussed.

"It's a tree all right," he said, looking up at the large, mangled maple that stood at the corner of Ellery and Mason. "A very big tree."

"It's my tree." Maggie patted the thick old trunk affectionately. "By the time I was ten years old I could climb to the top of it, and I was the only one who could, too. Boys included."

"I bet," Dunne said. He squinted upward again. "The top, huh? Are we, uh, going to the top tonight?"

"What's the matter?" Maggie teased. "Chicken?"

"Never!" Dunne said manfully. "Lily-livered sometimes. Yellow-bellied often. But never chicken."

"Come on." Maggie swung herself onto the lowest branch, grabbed the one above it with her hands, and began to pull herself up. "Just follow me. Use your bare hands, and don't look down. If you have to fall, fall to your right."

"Fall to my right?" Below her, Dunne sounded mystified.

"Leaves." Maggie gestured carelessly downward. "There's a big pile of leaves down there. I raked them myself and jumped in them just a few days ago."

"What were you doing raking leaves in a vacant lot?"

"I just told you," Maggie said. "I wanted to jump in them. So did half the kids in the neighborhood. There are a lot of trees around this lot. You can make a really good leaf-jumping pile."

"Right," Dunne said. "You, lady, are stark, raving nuts."

Maggie's laughter reverberated among the rough-barked branches. "I always used to love to do this," she said, climbing higher. "When I was a child I'd get to feeling that I knew everybody and everything that had ever happened in West Haven, and that nothing had ever been exciting here, and that nothing ever would be. And I'd want to run away from home, but I couldn't. That's when I'd come here and climb all the way to the top, and everything would be perfect."

"Where did you want to run away to?" Dunne asked.

The top branch was just above her, and Maggie pulled herself up, holding tightly to the trunk until she could sit. She looked out over the houses of Mason and Ellery and Noble Streets and breathed deeply.

"Take that branch right across from me," she told Dunne, motioning with her foot. "And remember, if you fall, push away from the tree. Fall right."

Dunne got what looked like a precarious seat on his branch. "You still haven't told me where you wanted to run to," he said.

"Paris," Maggie sighed. "I wanted to go to Paris."

"Why Paris?"

She shrugged, a little embarrassed by her childhood dreams. "I used to read all these writers, Hemingway, Fitzgerald, Colette. They'd all lived in Paris. Wonderful things always seemed to happen in Paris. Love, especially. The women in Colette's novels always had dozens of people in love with them."

Dunne wrapped his arm around the tree trunk to get a better grip. "Why didn't you go when you ran away at seventeen?" he asked. "Why did you go to California?"

Maggie hesitated. This was delicate territory. "I went to California because I could get a job there," she said slowly. "As a secretary. I took typing and shorthand as well as college courses in high school. I got a job with a movie agent. It all seemed very glamorous at the time."

"You could have saved your money and gone to Paris then," Dunne suggested.

"Maybe," Maggie admitted. "Maybe I even intended to."

"Am I allowed to ask a personal question?"

"Such as?"

"Such as who the guy was and what he did to you?"

"Am I really that transparent?" Maggie asked, feeling warmed by the gruff, almost angrily protective tone in which Dunne had asked the question. "I thought I was doing a good job of playing the gay, unbitter divorcée."

"You're doing a good job of erecting a castle keep around your head," Dunne said dryly. "Are you telling me you married this—this person?" He sounded as if he would have preferred to use a stronger word.

"Hamlin Robert Marshall." Maggie tried to keep her tone light. "I was married to him for four years. When I first met you, I thought you were a lot like him."

"Oh, fine."

"No," Maggie insisted. "In some ways you are a lot like him. He was a very forceful person. And, like you, he could be very charming."

"You didn't leave him because he was charming,"

Dunne pointed out. "Or did he leave you?"

"I left him," Maggie said firmly. "I left him because he was—he wasn't really very good at anything, you see. He got people to do things for him. He got *me* to do things for him. And he liked it that way. He—" Maggie paused and took a deep breath. "I'd never intended to be a career woman; I believed in a traditional marriage. But after I divorced Ham I needed to prove to myself that there was a world where achievement mattered. So I came back and took a job in the Daystar typing pool, I looked around at things I thought I'd like to do in the company, and when I made up my mind to go into the design department, I went back to school part time to get my degree."

"And did very well," Dunne complimented her. "I checked that, too. You have a better scholastic record than ninety percent of the employees in the department."

"That and a quarter will get me a cup of coffee," Maggie said sardonically.

"Maybe forty cents," Dunne agreed. "I'll even sit here and admit something that would scandalize my lawyers: You probably have a point about the design department. If I'd been running the company myself these last few years—"

"What do you mean, *if* you'd been running the company yourself?" Maggie demanded. "I thought you owned Daystar."

"I do," Dunne assured her. "But Daystar isn't all I do. I'm starting a computer leasing business out in Las Vegas. For the past four or five years I've been putting together a corporation that will handle the design of various kinds of academic programs—publish the books, handle the visual aids, compile bibliographies of outside reading, even propose total-environment games."

"The past four or five years!" Maggie yelped indignantly. "How could you!"

"Maggie!" Dunne cautioned in alarm. "Maggie, calm down. You're going to fall!"

"Don't tell me to calm down!" Maggie snapped, fuming. "You've spent the last four or five years putting together a corporation, have you? You weren't running Daystar at all?"

"Why am I getting the feeling that that simple little fact is going to be my death warrant? Maggie, don't push me!"

"Don't push you? Why not?" she asked wickedly, inching a little closer to him. She put her hand on the branch where he was seated and began to rock it, slowly and deliberately. "I remember a certain person"—she rocked with increasing force—"who treated me like a complete idiot because I didn't know he was the head of my company. Except it turns out there was no reason I *should* know he was head of my company, because during the time I've been with the company, he hasn't even been around. He's been off starting a corporation somewhere!"

"Maggie!" The panic was evident in Dunne's voice. "Maggie, in the first place, you aren't making any sense. In the second place, you're going to kill me. Stop rocking that branch!"

"All right," she said with deceptive agreeableness. "I'll stop rocking the branch. But I have to be leaving now." She swung herself around until she was hugging the trunk, then began to slide swiftly down, bouncing her feet against the branches as she reached them.

"Come on," she called to Dunne. "You want to hang around up there all alone?"

"Come back up here and tell me how to get down," Dunne demanded.

"Not a chance," Maggie chuckled.

"I didn't fall," Dunne said, sounding as surprised as if he'd just witnessed a miracle. He kicked gently at the pile of leaves under his feet, shaking his head in wonder. "I didn't fall," he repeated. "Remarkable."

Maggie threw herself backward into the leaf pile, glorying in the way it compressed into softness under her shoulders. She churned leaves into the air and watched them drift above her, mingling with the light snow and reflecting the glow of the street lamps.

"I knew you'd be all right," she told Dunne complacently, pleased at her minor revenge. "I love jumping in leaves, don't you? They always smell so clean."

Dunne looked dubious, but he took a hop from where he was standing and landed beside her in the pile. Then he propped himself up on one elbow and stared down into her face, his eyebrows arched in amusement.

"Lady, you're not just stark, raving mad. You're an alien. Remind me to ask you what planet you're from."

She ignored the comment. "I told you it was all right," she pointed out. "Bounce around a little. We've got three feet of leaves under us. It's softer than a mattress."

"I think I'd prefer the mattress," Dunne said wryly. He reached out to stroke her face with his fingertips, drawing imaginary circles against the soft skin of her cheeks. Maggie felt a shiver go through her that had nothing to do with the cold. Dunne seemed so close, so ready. The zipper of his jacket had come open at the neck, and she could see the hollow of his throat. All she had to do was reach out and she could touch him there.

"You're a funny woman, Margaret Mary Hennessy," he said softly, his fingers now traveling down the base of her jaw to her neck, then to her collarbone. "Climbing trees, falling in leaves, singing carols with senior citizens at the local church. Maybe you don't even exist. Maybe you're a figment of my imagination."

"Oh, I exist all right," she said weakly, butterflies rampaging en masse through her stomach. "I exist in the hundreds of thousands. There's a whole neighborhood full of Maggie Hennessys right here."

"No there isn't." Dunne kissed her eyelids, then let his lips travel down the side of her face in feathery caresses. "There's only one Margaret Mary Hennessy. I should know; I've looked."

"Maybe you've looked in all the wrong places," she said breathlessly.

"Of course I have," Dunne said. "I've never looked here."

He drew himself up until he was lying alongside her, his legs stretched against hers and his chest pressed against her heaving breasts. Suddenly Maggie longed to slide out of her garments, to feel the cold wind against her overheated skin.

"You're remarkable, Maggie Hennessy," Dunne murmured, his tongue darting out to trace a tantalizing whorl inside the delicate shell of her ear. "You're a walking mystery. Every time I look at you, you're different. I don't think I'm ever going to get enough of you."

"We're in a pile of leaves," she said softly. "In the middle of West Haven. In the cold."

"Do you really care?" Dunne teased.

"Not for the moment," she admitted, feeling sure the hot flush Dunne started in her would be enough to make her warm in the arctic. "But later—"

"Let's worry about later when it comes," Dunne urged. "Just lie beside me now. Let me feel you against me, and let yourself want me. I want you so much, it's like pain."

His hands worked their way inside her jacket and began to stroke her arms, her waist, her ribs, and then the soft mounds of her breasts. Maggie could feel his fingers working over the wool of her sweater, tracing delicate circles that made her feel as if she would burst. She reached inside his jacket and massaged the broad expanse of his back, wanting to feel his bare skin and being frustrated by the soft material of his shirt.

"Let's go back to my house," she suggested. "We'll be out of the cold."

"Let's stay right here." Dunne laughed gently as he nuzzled her neck. Then he found an electric area of vulnerability at the top of her spine, and Maggie felt a stream of fire coursing through her body, singeing her yet making her long for more.

"Inside," Maggie pleaded again.

"Right here," Dunne caught her hair in his hands, and his lips sought hers. "Let me show you what we can have right here, right now. Let me show you that anything is possible for the two of us, Maggie. Anything."

Maggie wrapped her arms around his neck and held him closer. She no longer felt the cold or the dampness of the powdery snow. She felt only the heat they were making between them.

Chapter Eight

THERE WERE LEAVES and snowflakes and small gusts of wind. Most of all there was the hot white light of unrealized desire flooding her bloodstream like lava. Her breasts heaved. Her lips parted in anticipation. Her hands came up to touch and then...

... nothing. Nothing happened.

Maggie looked down at the pile of blueprints on the floor at her feet. She'd come to Bidemeyer that morning meaning to check the placement of the obstacles in The Game—she was sure one or two of the great flat rocks in the North Meadow were right in the path of an escape route—but she hadn't been able to concentrate. All she could think about was Dunne—first that astounding hour in the leaves, then the long walk home, the chaste kiss on the cheek, the sound of the Alfa Romeo as it drove off. He'd ended the evening being the perfect gentleman, not pressing his obvious advantage at all. She'd been more than warm when they were lying in that soggy pile of leaves in the open air, but when she heard the sound of Dunne's car fading in the distance, she'd begun to feel the cold.

Quickly she picked up a set of blueprints and began pinning them to the bulletin board, smoothing them flat before she anchored them. She was being silly. Of course nothing had happened. She hadn't wanted it to. Getting involved that way with Dunne Holborn would be a disaster. Even if he turned out to be a saint—and she was willing to admit he was probably a far better person than she'd first thought him—she still wouldn't be able to handle him. As soon as she let down her guard, he'd walk all over her. She'd been used as a rug before.

Besides, Maggie thought, scooping up another set of blueprints and continuing her tacking, her shakiness this morning was just nerves from lack of sleep. When she actually saw Dunne she'd be calm, cool, and professional. She'd behave as if the previous night had never happened.

The phone rang, and she nearly jumped out of her skin, pins and blueprints falling everywhere. She dived for the phone, her hands shaking. What if Dunne didn't want to act as if the previous night had never happened? What then?

"Hennessy," she barked into the receiver.

"Maggie?" Cass's voice sounded faint and far away. "Where have you been? I called about six times last night."

Maggie could hardly keep the relief out of her voice. "I was out late," she said. "I didn't get in till around one."

"I won't ask what there is to do in West Haven at one o'clock in the morning," Cass said. "I don't want to know." For a moment Maggie was afraid Cass would probe into her activities of the night before. Cass would know that Advent parties at St. Stephen's didn't go on as late as one in the morning.

But Cass had other things on her mind. "Listen," she said, "I've got a surprise for you. We've had a little... event in the case."

"Event?" Maggie was puzzled. "I thought you had the whole thing figured out. I didn't think anything could surprise you."

"What I've got could surprise Perry Mason," Cass declared. "About five-thirty last night I got a visitor. Her name is Sheila Frame. Ever hear of her?"

"No," Maggie said.

"She'd never heard of you, either. At least not until yesterday. She works in the executive office of Daystar, over on Orange Street."

"Nobody from Design ever knows anybody from Executive," Maggie said. "The two buildings are half a city apart."

"She explained all that," Cass said hurriedly. "That's not the point. The point is that she's boiling mad. She's been with Daystar seven years, she's making less than men who've been hired last week, she's had to train her last two bosses, and she works with one idiot who pinches her rear every morning. He's two grades above her on the hierarchy, makes twice what she does, and has half her education and training. She wants to quit, and she wants to sue."

"I don't blame her," Maggie said.

"The story isn't finished," Cass went on. "Yesterday morning the idiot—the one who pinches her—tried to put his hand down her dress. She scratched up his face, told him what she thought of him, and went back to her desk to clear out. Then she decided to do one last thing for the cause. She'd been keeping a lot of documentation on the things that had been happening, and she picked it all up and marched down the hall to one of the top execs and bawled *him* out. She showed him all her evidence and told him she was going to sue. And guess what he said."

"I don't think I'll guess," Maggie said cautiously.

"Good. You couldn't. He told her not to quit, but he said she *ought* to sue. Told her she had every right. And he sent her to me. Now, just guess who pulled that little number."

Maggie sighed. "I suppose it was Dunne Holborn," she said resignedly.

"Got it in one," Cass said with satisfaction. "Now, you tell me, why would our glamour boy pull a stunt like that?"

Maggie made a hopeful but foredoomed guess. "Because Dunne Holborn is an honest and honorable man conscientiously attempting to act in good faith?" she offered bravely.

"Try selling me some wooden nickels," Cass snorted.

"But, Cass..." Maggie began, about to make the mistake of telling her friend that when she'd seen Dunne the night before, he hadn't mentioned a word about this Sheila Frame. Then there was a knock on the door and the sound of the knob turning. By the time Cass had hung up—without bothering to say good-bye—Dunne was ushering a short, fat little man into Maggie's office.

Maybe it was because it all happened so fast, or because she hadn't had a chance to assimilate Cass's information about Sheila Frame, or because she still hadn't been able to stop thinking about the night before. Maggie wasn't sure. She only knew that seeing Dunne was even worse than she'd expected it to be. At the sight of his broad-shouldered body filling her doorway, Maggie felt her throat tighten and her skin begin to tingle. She tried to tear her eyes away from him but couldn't—which was unfortunate, because those two emerald orbs were glinting in intimate amusement, making Maggie feel exposed and vulnerable.

Then Dunne stepped forward, guiding the chubby little man along with him. It almost broke the mood, but not quite.

"Ms. Hennessy," Dunne said, the formality of his voice belying the intimacy of his glance. "This is Mr. Bartholomew, president of the L-Star Society."

Maggie turned hastily toward the official, happy to have something other than Dunne to concentrate on. What was he up to, anyway? Was he trying to unnerve her again, to make her stumble in front of the client? Or had he, too, been unable to stop thinking of their evening together?

Maggie wasn't sure she wanted to know. She held out her hand to Mr. Bartholomew and smiled. "I'm glad to meet you," she said in her most professional voice. "I've met a number of your members, and I must admit, you're the first one I've seen in a business suit."

Bartholomew laughed. "I'll even wear a business suit at the conference," he confessed. "I'm going to sit in the office and oversee the activities with the rest of the umpires. I'm an animator. That's enough fantasy in anyone's life without adding antennae to it."

"Oh, dear," Maggie chuckled. "I was getting rather fond of antennae!" Bartholomew looked pleased at that remark, and Maggie began to relax. As long as she kept her eyes off Dunne, she could control herself. All she had to do was focus on Mr. Bartholomew.

She put the blueprints she'd been holding into a neat, orderly pile on the desk. "Did you come for the grand tour?" she asked the man. "We're right in the middle of setup, so I'm afraid things are a little complicated. . . ."

"There's a problem with some of the equipment for the StarRiders," Dunne interposed smoothly, coming around the desk to stand beside her, so that they were both facing Bartholomew. The sleeve of Dunne's suit jacket brushed lightly against her arm, and Maggie almost jumped. "Mr. Bartholomew seems to think the equipment we received is defective."

"Oh, dear," Maggie murmured, edging imperceptibly

away from Dunne. He was trying to get her rattled, she was sure of it. Her jaw set in determination. No matter what had—or hadn't—happened between them, she wasn't ever going to let him fluster her in a business situation again.

"If the equipment is here, maybe we should go see it," she told Mr. Bartholomew pleasantly. "There isn't much time before the game, you know. If we send equipment back, we may not receive replacements in time. With any luck it's something we can fix here."

Mr. Bartholomew nodded eagerly. "Dunne, here, said he was sure you could handle it," he declared. "I don't care how we solve it, but it's got to be solved. I find it very troubling when something goes wrong this close to opening."

"So do I," Maggie affirmed. "Why don't you go on upstairs and I'll find my game plans and join you. Then we can get right to work."

Maggie started rummaging in her desk as the two men headed out the door, Bartholomew with brisk optimism, Dunne reluctantly. She waited only long enough to be sure they had made headway down the corridor, then grabbed the two-hundred-page master game plan from the bottom drawer and hurried out behind them. She caught up with them when they were halfway to the stairs.

"What are you trying to do?" she hissed in Dunne's ear, hoping her voice was too low for Bartholomew to hear.

"Do?" The look on Dunne's face was too innocent to be believed. "Actually, the only thing I was thinking of doing was making a bet with you."

Maggie was about to retort that that wasn't what she was talking about, but his expression intrigued her. "What kind of bet?" she asked slowly, still keeping her voice low and grateful that Mr. Bartholomew was charging on ahead of them.

Dunne nearly broke into laughter. "About these spear guns of Bartholomew's. He'll tell us what's going wrong.

You try to fix them, and I'll write my solution on a piece of paper. Best solution wins."

"But you've got a head start," Maggie protested.

Dunne shook his head. "All I know is that the spear guns won't fire properly. I haven't looked them over. I don't know any more than you do."

Maggie bit her lip. On the surface the notion was intriguing, although she had no idea why Dunne was proposing it. Maybe she'd be able to show him up for a change. After all the confusion he'd caused her since he came into her life, he deserved his comeuppance. Still, she didn't remember many details about the spear guns herself. What if she wasn't able to come up with a solution?

Quickly she made a decision. "All right," she said. "But if I win, I want a solemn declaration from you that I know my job and I'm good at it."

"Of course," Dunne said lightly. "And if you win, I'll give you the day off and take you somewhere wonderful."

Maggie was already hurrying forward to catch up with Bartholomew before she realized how Dunne had twisted his words. She still had no idea what would happen if she *lost*.

"Right through here," Maggie said as she caught up to the L-Star president. She took the man's arm and began to steer him through a low doorway. "As Mr. Holborn undoubtedly told you, we've reserved this floor of this wing for equipment and costumes. We've given the StarRiders their own room because there are so many of them?"

"It must be wonderful making your living like this," Bartholomew sighed as Maggie switched on the overhead lights. "I spend a lot of my time drawing things like little tiny mushrooms. Over and over again."

"It isn't always like this," Maggie informed him. "Special projects are a wonderful treat for everyone, but we'd never make enough money to stay in business if they were all we did. We do a lot of things over and over again, too, like mass-produced role-playing games."

"Board games?" Bartholomew asked in confusion.

Maggie shook her head. "Information packets," she explained. "There's no set action in a Daystar game. In our economics game, Takeover, there are packets for four fictitious corporations, the SEC, and the Antitrust Division of the U.S. Department of Justice. Each student picks a role, gets the packet for that role, then goes off and does whatever he or she thinks he can get away with. Let the best man, woman, or team win."

"And you mass-produce these things?"

"We mass-produce the structures for some highly sophisticated role-playing," Maggie said. "These structures are what we call games. The teaching games are packaged and sold to schools and colleges all across the country, and they're updated every six months. A lot of us spend a lot of time—"

"Drawing mushrooms," Bartholomew offered.

"It's at least as bad." Maggie grinned, then looked around the small, cramped room. "Now, what seems to be the problem here?" she asked.

"I think Mr. Bartholomew said the spear guns were misfiring," Dunne put in politely.

Maggie looked up and saw him standing in the doorway. He must have been there for some time but she hadn't noticed him. She wished she could have continued in blissful ignorance of his potent presence. He was still shooting her veiled looks, and she was still much too disturbed by his presence.

Besides, he was directly challenging her.

Maggie quickly scanned the room. The StarRiders were a group she herself had invented specifically for use in this game. Any of the players could sign up and become one, and many had decided to do so. She'd also designed all the equipment, including the spear guns, but it was so long ago—back in the earliest planning stages—that she scarcely remembered a thing about them.

She was trying to think hopeful thoughts when her eyes fell on a stack of long, tubelike objects in a far corner. Those were the spear guns. She went across the room and picked one up. "Well, here they are. Rayzars, I think I named them."

"That's right." Bartholomew hurried forward. "We got samples of all the equipment up at Headquarters, you know, and when we tried these out, well, you shoot them about four times, and then they stop. They just don't work anymore!"

Maggie turned the tube over and over in her hands, trying not to look at Dunne as she did so. He'd seen the same thing she had, and he was clearly amused. The Rayzars bore the stamp of the Acme Novelty Company, a cheap outfit whose extensive inventory of joke items included more than a few whose active lives were shorter than the time it took to purchase them. Normally, Daystar never dealt with Acme. This time, however, the unreliable company was the only one willing to make the Rayzars at the limited cost she had specified. Obviously it hadn't made them very well.

Maggie handed the tube to Dunne and tried to ignore his intense scrutiny of the weapon. "They shoot about four times and then don't work anymore," she mused aloud. "How many did you try out?"

"All six of the Rayzars I got at Headquarters," Bartholomew promptly replied. "One shot three times and quit. One made it all the way to ten. The other four shot four times and quit."

Maggie fit one of the cushion-tipped Styrofoam "spears" into the tube she was holding and fired. She fitted and fired four more times. On the sixth attempt she felt something in her hand snap and knew the trigger connection inside the mechanism had broken. The Rayzar wouldn't fire at all.

She put the spear gun carefully on the floor. There were two things she knew she couldn't do: She couldn't send the Rayzars back to Acme to be replaced, and she couldn't get the staff to fix the guns themselves. Acme was likely to send more defective equipment or none at all. Fixing the spear guns at the site would take too much time. She tried to ignore Dunne's furtive but furious scribbling on a piece of paper. This time she was undaunted by his intelligence, expertise, and force of character. Even if God Himself came down from the heavens and showed Dunne the correct way to fix the trigger connection, there still wouldn't be time to alter all three hundred guns.

Suddenly Maggie had an idea. She grabbed her copy of the game plan and began to flip wildly through the pages.

"What we want to do here is find a solution that will allow us to begin on schedule and that can't mess us up in the middle, right?" she asked Bartholomew.

Bartholomew nodded.

"Given your budget, it would probably be a good idea to find something that won't cost any money, too," Maggie continued. "Fortunately, I invented the StarRiders. No one but the staff knows much about them yet. People know the StarRiders are supposed to be mercenary soldiers, but that's about it. So"—she pushed her copy of the master plan at Bartholomew—"what we do is write the malfunction into the game."

"What?"

It was really two "What?"'s—one from Bartholomew and one from Dunne, who had looked up from his scribbling to stare at her in what looked like shock and admiration combined. Maggie felt a wave of pride and triumph surging through her. She'd managed to beat Dunne Holborn at his own game—she was sure of it! Nothing he'd written down on that miserable piece of paper could possibly be as good as her solution.

She bent closer to Bartholomew. "I'm going to run this through the computer, but what we do is turn the faulty mechanism into one of the StarRider's limitations. They're all armed, you see, but they never know how long that will last, so they're going to have to plan for it."

Half an hour later, after giving Mr. Bartholomew a complete tour of the Bidemeyer House, Maggie and Dunne stood at the front door, watching the L-Star president stuff his roly-poly frame into a hired black Lincoln Continental. She felt exhilarated. She'd never before been faced with such a head-on challenge to her abilities, and she never would have believed she'd be able to meet it so well. The experience gave her new confidence.

She shut the door on the cold and the rain and turned to the grinning, enticing man beside her.

"Well?" she demanded, her hands on her hips. "Aren't you going to tell me what a genius I am?"

"Genius is putting it mildly," Dunne said with a laugh. "I'd never have thought of that kind of solution. I went right for the mechanical problem. You're a smart lady, Maggie Hennessy. Not that I ever doubted it."

"No?" Maggie asked shrewdly. "Then what was this all about? Not just the challenge—everything."

Dunne didn't even try to deny the strange way he'd been treating her all morning. "'Everything' is my inability to keep from smiling when I look at you. After last night..." He shook his head. "You may be able to stay perfectly controlled around me after what happened, but I can't be that way around you. I don't think I even want to."

"Nothing happened," Maggie blurted. Then embarrassed, she hurried on, ignoring Dunne's raised eyebrows. "You almost made me laugh at poor Mr. Bartholomew," she scolded him. "If you had, I'd have broken your ankle."

"No more attacks on my ankles, please." Dunne grinned. "And you behaved like a perfect professional. You can congratulate yourself on that. As for the challenge..." He shrugged. "I've never seen you work before, you know. This seemed like the fastest way I could think of to find out what you were made of. You're not mad about that, are you?"

"No," Maggie admitted. "It was exciting. And I won, so I guess I really can't complain. But don't you think it would have been easier just to read my game plan from start to finish? You're going to have to get around to it someday, you know. You're supposed to be on site for the convention."

"I'll get around to it," Dunne promised. "But being chief designer requires more than being able to write a good game plan. There's a lot of day-to-day administration. I had to see for myself, Maggie. We've got a lawsuit to deal with."

Maggie frowned. She was feeling much too good to think about the lawsuit now. Not that she didn't want to pursue the suit—a few days with Dunne Holborn, no matter how charming, didn't make up for five years of humiliation at the hands of his employees—but she didn't want it getting in the way of the overwhelming feelings of triumph the last few hours had given her.

Suddenly something else occurred to her. In the excitement of the challenge, she'd almost forgotten about it.

"Dunne," she asked slowly, "what about Sheila Frame?"

"Sheila Frame?" For a few moments Dunne's expression was blank. Then recognition dawned on him. "Cass must have called you." He nodded. "I suppose I do owe you an explanation for that." He looked restlessly around the foyer. "I promised you two things if you won: a statement of your expertise and an afternoon off with a trip to someplace wonderful. Remember?"

"I don't know if I have time for a trip to someplace wonderful," Maggie said. "Besides, what does that have to do with Sheila Frame?"

"You've got time for a day off if I say you do," Dunne said authoritatively. "Come on, get your coat. When we get there, I'll tell you all about Sheila Frame—and everything else."

Maggie hesitated, but Dunne was obviously in no mood to take no for an answer. He grabbed her coat from the rack near the door and dropped it into her arms.

"Give me a minute to bring the car around from the back," he said. "It's pretty wet out there."

He was halfway out the door when he remembered something, fished around in the pocket of his jacket, and came back to hand Maggie a piece of paper.

"My solution." He grinned, then disappeared.

Maggie looked down at the paper in her hand. She really couldn't afford the time off, but when Dunne wanted to be persuasive, he could be irresistible. Which was exactly his danger to her. But for some reason, right at that moment she didn't feel like fighting him. Would she ever feel like fighting him again? Or if she stayed around him for long, would she cease to exist as a person and just fade into the woodwork? She thought of Ham and shuddered. Then she remembered her feeling of triumph after the challenge and relaxed slightly. Maybe she did have it in her to hold her own with a man like Dunne.

She began doing up her coat, hastily shoving her arms through the sleeves and pulling at the buttons with nervous fingers. She shouldn't even let herself think those thoughts. She knew what life was like with a man who was used to having his own way all the time. She'd had four years of it, and she never wanted to try it again.

She was on her way to the door when she realized she still had Dunne's solution crushed into a ball in her right hand. Curiously she unwadded the paper. It showed step-by-step instructions on how to fix the trigger mechanism, complete wtih diagrams.

Good heavens, she thought. Dunne Holborn had to be some kind of mechanical genius.

Chapter Nine

THE BUILDING AT the end of the long, winding drive that curved up the hill wasn't a house at all; it was a mansion. Maggie fiddled with her seat belt, trying not to stare as Dunne went through the intricate process of getting the Alfa Romeo to stop, park, and stand still. She'd never seen anything as large and impressive as this two-story Georgian dream with its perfectly balanced twenty-foot-high front windows and graceful, sloping roof. Even in California, where Hamlin and his friends had been so obsessed with having the biggest and most expensive of anything that could be bought, no one she knew would have dreamed of possessing such quiet elegance. Whoever lived there had been too rich and too well connected for too long to feel a need to prove anything to anybody.

Dunne finally turned toward her, grabbing her hand.

"Come on," he said. "You've got to ring the door-bell."

"Ring the doorbell?" she asked, confused. But Dunne had already gotten out and was hurrying around the front of the car to get her door for her. Maggie let him help her out onto the wet pavement.

"Go on, pull the doorbell," Dunne said eagerly.

"*Pull* the doorbell?" Maggie asked.

"It's the old-fashioned kind," Dunne explained.

Maggie did as she was told. The bellpull seemed to stick, so she tugged a little harder. It gave abruptly, and Maggie found herself first stepping back, then regaining her balance, then being showered with blue, green, and yellow feathers. The feathers were so unexpected, she shrieked. "What is this stuff?" she demanded. "It's smothering me!"

"You've got a feather up your nose." Dunne chuckled. "But this is nothing. Inside it throws confetti."

"Does it make a bell ring?" Maggie asked wryly, stepping back.

"Only if you push the button on top of the knob," Dunne admitted. "I made that when I was twelve years old—with some help from my father—and nearly gave my Uncle Donald a heart attack. You see, we'd always had the pull, and then we got the button bell, but Uncle Don didn't know about the button, so—"

"Never mind," Maggie said hastily. "I get the picture. Your father let you do something like this to this beautiful old house?"

"That's not all he let me do," Dunne said proudly. He fished keys out of his pocket and fitted them into the lock. "Enter, madame. Just watch out for the confetti."

Maggie hesitated, reluctant to step inside. She had the same feeling about this house that she often did about very expensive glassware—that it would break if she touched it. She simply wasn't used to such luxury. "Did you grow up here?" she asked, postponing the moment when she would have to venture indoors.

"I grew up here," Dunne confirmed. "My father grew up here. Even my grandfather grew up here."

"My grandfather grew up in County Cork," Maggie said, grinning, "and something tells me that even there he didn't have a place like this. If he had, he never would have moved."

"Don't be too sure of that," Dunne murmured.

"I'm sure of it," Maggie said. "If I got my hands on a place like this, you wouldn't be able to get me out with a pickax. Really, Dunne, it's the most beautiful place I've ever seen. It's even lovelier than Bidemeyer."

"Smaller than Bidemeyer, but with advantages," Dunne said. "Come on, I've got a lot to show you. I spent eighteen years of my life in this house, and I made the most of them."

Maggie let him draw her into the large foyer.

"Boo," she said aloud, trying to allay what she knew were silly fears.

The sound echoed hollowly through the huge, almost empty vestibule. Maggie glanced uneasily around. Against one wall was a low, mirrored table with a quasimodernistic brass sculpture on its marble top. There was a coatrack—also brass, also modernistic, and obviously expensive—in one corner. Otherwise the foyer was empty.

"How do you like it?" Dunne asked, coming up behind her.

"Very elegant," Maggie said, trying to sound enthusiastic. "Your mother didn't believe in furniture, I take it."

Dunne sighed. "I've put a lot of things into storage and a lot more under dustcovers. I don't live here, you know. I just keep it for sentimental reasons."

Maggie stared at him, stunned. "You have a beautiful place like this and don't live in it?" she demanded. "Why not?"

"Well, for one thing, it's too big for me. It's got forty rooms, after all. What would I do with them all? Also"—

he looked around a bit uneasily and shrugged—"I feel sort of ambivalent about it, I guess. My parents were good people—with all his money, my father still had a genius for woodworking, and he enjoyed passing it on— and I was happy, but I was alone a great deal. When I come back here to look after the, uh, projects, I always end up feeling rather lost and sorry for myself. In fact, if so much of the stuff I made as a child wasn't literally built right into the walls, I'd probably sell the place tomorrow."

"You mean there are more things like the doorbell?" Maggie asked.

"Dozens," Dunne promised.

"I can hardly wait," she said faintly.

Dunne grinned and ushered her into a living room that looked big enough to be a basketball court. In a way it was cold and unwelcoming. Beige drapes and white curtains hung from the tops of the floor-to-ceiling windows. Beige modular furniture, wrapped in plastic dustcovers, was strewn artfully across the thick-piled beige carpet. Maggie wrinkled her nose in distaste. To her, beige wasn't so much neutral as nonexistent. It said nothing to her.

What did say something were the myriad useful and fanciful objects built into the walls, the tables, and even the floor. One of the bland modular chairs suddenly sprouted arms when sat in. A cigarette lighter hidden in a hand-carved hoot owl sprung from the floor when activated by a pedal hidden just under the carpet near the coffee table. The coffee table itself had several secret drawers. Maggie was afraid to lean against anything. Everything she touched seemed to set off some kind of improbable chain reaction.

"My father not only had a genius for woodworking, he had a genius for practical jokes," Dunne said, laughing. "So did I. And I didn't have his restraint, either. Want to see the ghost in the gallery?"

"There's a ghost in the gallery?" Maggie asked.

"Come see," Dunne urged. He grabbed her hand and led her up a long set of stairs. She noticed a few light spots on the wall where pictures had been, and a few oddly carved newel posts that might have been more "practical jokes," but most of the decor went by in a blur.

"I made this when I was fifteen," Dunne was saying. "I'd just started getting interested in engines, in electricity. My father was committed to working in wood. He didn't like what he called "machines." Of course, almost everything he and I built into this house was a machine—not electrical, but machines nonetheless—but he didn't like metal or motors. When I found out later what you could do with a rotary motor and half a dollar's worth of gasoline, I didn't know how to contain myself. It was magic. The only thing I've ever found more magical than that was when I first realized what could be done with a computer. That wasn't just magic; that was a miracle."

He pulled her onto a long balcony over a large reception room—what Maggie recognized from her reading of Daphne du Maurier as a minstrel's gallery.

"My mother used to hold charity luncheons down there," Dunne said. "The effect is really a lot better from the floor. I had a whole pack of those social ladies in hysterics one afternoon—a very rainy afternoon, by the way. It tends to look better in the dark. My mother nearly killed me. Watch."

Maggie didn't see Dunne push a button or pull a lever to start the mechanism, but she did hear the initial whir and the throaty, deathlike chuckles that followed it. In the dark, empty house with the rain coming down outside, the otherworldly rasps gave her a clammy feeling in the palms of her hands and a tingling in her scalp. Maggie had never been fond of ghost stories. She found herself becoming less and less fond of them as the eerie noises grew louder. Then something seemed to move at the end of the gallery, and a gray and red figure with long, matted hair, waving a broom, popped out of the darkness.

Maggie turned and ran. The minstrel's gallery intersected with a long corridor lined on either side with doors. She ducked into the first of these and groped for the light switch.

The room she had entered was a perfect octagon, bordered on seven sides by stained-glass windows and on the eighth by the door she had just come in through. Pale sunlight filtered through the colored panes, splashing a riotous rainbow over the bare wooden floor. The furniture was exquisitely carved of the best materials. The antique vanity table with its beveled mirrors was of fine old cherrywood. The low daybed was covered with an intricate patchwork quilt.

Maggie heard Dunne come up behind her and turned. "What is this place?" she asked him. "It's like something out of a fairy tale."

Dunne glided into the room and sat down on the daybed. "There are a lot of strange rooms in a house like this. Heaven only knows what they were used for originally. When I was young, I liked to think that the architect who built this house was a lot like me—that he liked to do intricate, complicated things just for the fun of it."

"You still like to do intricate, complicated things," Maggie chided. "Only now you like to play with computers and design total-environment games."

Dunne laughed. "All right," he said. "And I still like to play with wood machines. You should see the place where I live. When I built it, I didn't have my father restraining my enthusiasm, and I didn't have to deal with the limitations of Georgian architecture. I got to do everything I wanted to."

"I don't think I'm ready for that," Maggie said.

"Of course you are," Dunne said easily. "Your work for Daystar. My house is just an extension of Daystar.

My life is just an extension of Daystar, really. I've never gotten over that first enthusiasm, you know. I love inventing things, putting together games, and putting together companies." He treated her to a long, appraising look. "What about you, Maggie? What do you like to do? What engages your total attention?"

Maggie walked slowly over to the daybed and sat down, musing. What Dunne had said about his interest in machines and games and companies sounded wonderful but completely outside her experience.

"It's not that way with me," she explained carefully. "It's not so much what I want to do as how I want to be. After I got divorced I didn't want to be a lawyer or a mathematician or a nuclear physicist. I wanted to be independent and successful and competent. When I went to work at Daystar I looked around for something I could be independent and successful and competent at. Do you see what I mean?"

Dunne nodded tentatively. "In a way. But was it always like that, even when you were young?"

"Oh, when I was young." Maggie waved her hand dismissively. "In Irish families the girls have two choices—or they did then: marriage or the convent. I didn't really think about things much when I was young, except for Paris, and that never seemed real. Except"—Maggie hesitated—"do you know White's?"

"The clothing store across from Vanderbilt at Yale?" Dunne looked surprised.

But Maggie nodded vigorously. "When Cass and I were in high school, there was a display in the window there. It was winter, Christmas, and they had this tweed skirt and cashmere sweater on one of those armless, headless forms. That seemed to pinpoint the whole thing for me—being a lady, having money, and going to Paris. Am I making any sense?"

"Not really," Dunne replied. "I guess I've never thought about the way I wanted to be, only the things I wanted to do. Besides"—he leaned forward and cupped her chin in his hands—"as far as I can tell, you *are* independent and competent, and at least on your way to being successful. And you're as ladylike as anyone could want to be." He grinned. "In public, anyway. In the leaves . . ."

"Don't remind me about the leaves," Maggie groaned.

"Why not?" Dunne demanded. He released her chin and slipped his hands around her waist, drawing her closer. "Ladylike, businesslike, professional—you have to be that way in public and on the job, but it would be a shame to carry it over into your private life." His teeth nipped gently, provocatively, at her ear.

"How do you think I should be in my private life?" Maggie asked, having to force amusement over the stirrings of her body. "A wanton hussy?"

"Try me," Dunne said eagerly. "I might love it."

"I might love it, too," Maggie admitted. Dunne's lips came down to nuzzle her neck, and she shivered with delight.

"Think of it as being independent, successful, and competent," Dunne said. "You're all those things, Maggie, and you're caring and concerned and involved in your world. Enjoy it."

"I can't enjoy it," Maggie muttered. "At the moment I can't even think about it."

"I'm not doing too well thinking myself at the moment," Dunne said with a chuckle.

His hands released her waist and slid up to grasp her shoulders. Maggie felt herself being lowered onto the smooth, plush surface of the quilt.

"I've been wanting to do this all day," Dunne murmured hoarsely. "Watching you work, watching you escort Bartholomew all over the site, listening to you being so cool and professional—it was making me crazy."

"I rather liked this afternoon." Maggie grinned. "I got a kick out of beating you."

"I should have thrown in the towel and carried you off on a white charger," Dunne said. His hands claimed her breasts, fingering the hardness of her nipples through the thin silk of her blouse. "Do you know where a man can get hold of a white charger these days?"

"Local knight shop," Maggie gasped, straining to stay in control long enough to respond to his banter. It was impossible. Bolts of electricity seemed to shoot through her every time he touched her, and her breath was coming in short, ragged gasps. "Armor at half price..." she started to say.

Then Dunne's tongue slipped into her mouth, teasing the hollows there. Maggie twisted on the quilt until she was lying alongside his broad chest, her hands free to discover him. She slipped her fingers through the front of his stiff white shirt, caressing the forest of soft, curling hair there. Her fingers traveled to his back and the knobby ridge of his spine. He stiffened against her and moaned, and she felt a heady thrill at the knowledge that she could arouse him as fully as he aroused her.

"I'll have to take retaliatory action for that," he whispered before his tongue came out to tease her ear. His fingers fumbled at the buttons of her blouse, pulling them open one by one and then pushing aside the flimsy constraint of her bra.

"You're so perfect," he said huskily, gazing down at her in wonder. He tugged at the zipper on her skirt, jerking impatiently when it caught on a loose thread. Then his task was accomplished.

Maggie felt a flood of anticipation as Dunne slid the skirt over her legs, then began to stroke the smooth skin of her inner thighs with long, teasing caresses. She buried her face in the hollow of his neck, wanting to be closer to him, wanting to feel every molecule of her body become one with his.

"When we're together like this, I can't imagine anything more." Dunne gripped her tightly. "I can't imagine there being anything more. Oh, Maggie, Maggie, if only we could stay like this forever."

"But this is forever," Maggie said groggily, unable to

think past the pulsing desire that seemed to envelop her. "This is the only forever there is."

"Then this is the only forever I want to know," Dunne declared. He leaned away from her, quickly discarding his shirt and jacket and tie. "Remind me of this whenever I begin to act like a fool."

"Maybe we're acting like fools now," Maggie said.

Dunne reached for her, her hips, her thighs, his fingers traveling with inexorable slowness down the length of her. Maggie twisted again, this time trying to keep his passage unobstructed. She wanted to feel his hands on every part of her body. She brought her hands to his neck, finding the sensitive spot at the back.

Then she felt his fingers slip under the lacy top of her brief bikini panties, and the waves of an emotion stronger than any she'd ever felt began to wash over her like a turbulent sea. A pulsing had started deep inside her, battering against her like breakers against a rocky shore. She wound her arms around his neck and held him, needing a rock to anchor her in this storm of desire. Then he reached closer, to a deeper, more intimate part of her, to the very center of her response to him. Maggie felt something inside her surge up to meet his promise, then fall back, frustrated, incomplete.

"Oh, Dunne, Dunne, please," she pleaded, shuddering against him. "Dunne, please—now."

Chapter Ten

IT ENDED SO QUICKLY, so completely, that for a few moments Maggie didn't realize anything had changed. Her body was throbbing. Her heart was thudding painfully. Something deep inside her demanded release and completion, things only Dunne could give. Then her straining nerves began to register the utter stillness of the man beside her, and her skin began to cool.

Dunne's muscles were still tense, poised, ready, but his concentration was elsewhere. His arms slipped from her back and dropped to the surface of the small daybed. Maggie pulled away from him, feeling confused, angry, and frightened. What was going on? And what could it possibly mean? The questions beat against her heart and her hopes like hailstones against a fragile pane of glass.

"Beeper," Dunne said, sitting up with a violent sweep of motion. "Damn!"

"Beeper?" Maggie was confused. Then she heard it, an insistent, faraway sound coming from under Dunne's clothes.

She jerked upright, brushing the tangled black hair out of her eyes. "What difference does a beeper make?" she demanded. "You're not a doctor; you run a business!"

"It's only for emergencies," Dunne said, sounding frustrated and angry himself. "Something's probably gone very wrong at Bidemeyer. When you're running a convention like this, things can get out of hand very fast. There's a phone in my car. Let's go down and find out what's gone wrong."

"I know what's gone wrong," Maggie said despondently. She got to her feet, snatching at the clothes that now littered the floor. The mere act of looking at Dunne's bare, seductively muscled chest was too painful to be endured. Moments before she had been pressed against it, full of desire, full of hope. Now... She slipped her arms through the straps of her bra. "I don't understand how you can do something like this," she said, anger breaking through to mask her hurt. "One minute you were—were—" Her voice broke. She took a deep breath and got hold of herself. "If your objective was to make me feel like a complete fool, you've succeeded admirably."

His hand shot out and caught her by the wrist, gripping her with almost painful intensity. "I told you it was business," he snapped. "We'll go down and find out what it is. Maybe we'll even have to go out to Bidemeyer and fix it. But we've got all night after that, Maggie. Business comes first with me; I told you that. Don't think I don't want to make love to you, because I do. I want it more than anything in the world."

"And I want a peanut-butter-and-jelly sandwich," Maggie retorted, pulling on the rest of her clothing in short, angry jerks. "I don't understand what you mean when you say things, Dunne. If making love to me was what you really wanted, I certainly wasn't offering any

objections." She plucked her silk shirt from the edge of
the bed. "Maybe I *should* have objected."

"Maggie"—Dunne reached out for her—"would you
listen to me for a minute?"

"Please excuse me if I feel I've been listening to you
far too much!"

"Maggie, please." He stroked her hair. "I know that
from your point of view I'm behaving like a monster,
but I can't help it, really. Now that that thing has gone
off, I'll never be able to settle down until I answer it. I
told you how involved I get in all this, how involved
I've always been. Daystar means too much to me. When
there's a crisis, I have to do something about it."

"Business shouldn't mean that much to anybody,"
Maggie muttered.

"Come on," Dunne coaxed. "Let's go down to the car
and phone. We'll find out what this is about, we'll see
what we have to do, then we'll plan out the rest of the
night. Could you really rest comfortably, knowing that
somewhere out at Bidemeyer a full-scale disaster was
going on?"

"A full-scale disaster?" Maggie questioned, not really
believing him.

Dunne was firm. "If it wasn't a full-scale disaster,
they wouldn't have beeped me. They have orders."

Maggie looked around for her coat. The afternoon had
been ruined, and Dunne's behavior had given her a great
deal to think about—all of it bad. Right now all she
really wanted to do was get out of that room and out of
that house.

When they got outside, Maggie found it was later than
she had suspected, dark and cold, and sliding into night.
She got into the passenger side of the Alfa Romeo and
tucked herself into the bucket seat, wrapping her coat
tightly around herself to ward off the cold. She was still
angry and hurt, but the first rush of explosive fury was
spent. All she wanted was to go home and hide. She

didn't want Dunne's magic evening. At that moment she wasn't sure she wanted Dunne. He was pushing her around like a rag doll, putting his interests and concerns first, dismissing hers. She was having no better luck standing up to him than she had had with Ham.

Dunne climbed into the bucket seat beside her, reached forward to pull a blue plastic receiver from under the dashboard, and held it to his ear. She'd heard of phones in cars, of course, but she'd never actually seen one.

"What is it?" she asked, seeing Dunne's brow furrow in anger.

"Just tell them they can't do it," he barked into the phone. "It's entirely against the contract." He paused. "I don't care what they say, and where they're from is immaterial. It's freezing out."

"Dunne . . ." Maggie began.

He waved impatiently in her direction, then turned his face away to concentrate on his conversation. "Just give them a standing order," he told whomever was on the other end of the line. "Then move them. We've got a week and a half—yes, yes, I see that. . . . They're *what?* What in the name of—"

"Dunne," Maggie said, more forcefully this time. "If it's about L-Star—"

"I'll be there in half an hour," Dunne snapped. "And don't let them *do* anything." He slammed the receiver under the dashboard.

Maggie tried to control herself. Obviously whatever news Dunne had received had upset him terribly. If she just kept calm, she ought to be able to get him to tell her what it was.

"Don't you think you ought to let me know what's going on?" she prodded in her most soothing tone.

Dunne was in no mood to be soothed. "What do you think is going on?" he demanded, viciously grinding into first gear. "There's an emergency at Bidemeyer, naturally. Why I take on projects like this in the first place is beyond me."

"Projects like what?" Maggie asked. "Dunne, if it's L-Star—"

Ignoring her, Dunne popped the car into second before it really had a chance to get rolling. "Things like this make me crazy."

Maggie recognized the route without difficulty. The Tandem Road, the turn onto Elm Street, the long drive along the Connecticut River—she could find her way to Bidemeyer in her sleep. She dug her hands into the pockets of her coat, clenched her fists, and fumed. So it was supposed to be *her* project, was it? He was going to stay out and let her run things, was he? Well, if that was what he called letting her run things, she didn't want to know what he'd mean by usurping her authority!

They took the turn onto the Bidemeyer Estate itself, passing through the tall wrought-iron gates without stopping. Of course the guard wouldn't bother to stop Dunne Holborn's car, Maggie thought angrily. Dunne Holborn was lord of this particular manor, at least for the moment. He could come and go at will.

Maggie sat up a little straighter in her seat. Now, what was that? It looked like— She wasn't sure what it looked like. There was something that looked like a gigantic crystal ball, and something else that looked like a crescent moon with a star just inside the tip. Then there were ... bears. What looked like thousands of bears. *Teddy* bears.

Maggie felt herself relax a little. Ewoks. She knew about the Ewoks. But what were they doing there so early? They weren't expected for a least another week.

She tugged at Dunne's sleeve. "Those are the Ewoks," she tried to explain.

"I don't care if they're the English royal family," Dunne snapped. "These things are always more trouble than they're worth. Great publicity—"

"I understand all that," Maggie interrupted impatiently. "But the Ewoks are just—"

Dunne brought the car to a skidding stop at the curve

of the drive. "If you know so much about it, *you* do something," he bit out savagely. Then he kicked the door open and leaped onto the gravel. "I've been over this stuff fifty times with the L-Star people. They *know* better." He turned his back on her and hurried off.

Maggie grabbed at her door handle and scurried after him. "If you'll just listen to me," she insisted, "I doubt this is as much of a crisis as you think."

"Damn juvenile delinquents," Dunne muttered, ignoring her entirely. "I told L-Star when I took this project on that I wasn't going to let it turn into the kind of circus science fiction conventions usually turn into. I gave them strict instructions—"

"But, Dunne—" Maggie protested.

"College boys with nothing better to do," he said furiously. "Computer hackers. Space-war specialists. Just because they have a certain aptitude for messing around with computers—just because a few of them can write a decent short story taking place on the planet Zeb— they think they own the earth. Well—"

"Dunne, will you just slow *down*," Maggie jerked his arm violently. "If you'll give me two minutes to explain something to you—"

"I don't have two minutes," he argued. "I've got to go over there"—he pointed to the knot of teddy bears near the west wing of the mansion—"and ask them to take me to their leader."

Maggie sighed. "Wouldn't you at least like to know who they are, what they are, and what they probably want?"

"Why don't we let them speak for themselves?" Dunne countered.

He turned and strode away from her, his jaw set at a stubborn angle. Maggie had half a mind to let him go it alone. It would serve him right if she went back to the car and locked herself in. *That* would fix him. How dare he dismiss her that way? She was the one who'd been on this project from the beginning. He didn't know what he was doing!

Dunne stopped in front of a tall Ewok with horn-rimmed glasses and began gesticulating wildly. Maggie sighed again. Much as she would have liked to, she couldn't leave Dunne in the lurch. He might be dismissing her professional credentials out of hand for the moment, but pretending he was right in his assessment of her abilities wouldn't help matters. The only thing she could do was wade in and try to straighten things out.

She started advancing on the cluster on Ewoks.

"...probably against the laws of the state of Connecticut," Dunne was insisting. "I can't have you burning—"

"Ms. Hennessy." It was the tall, bespectacled Ewok who spoke. He came forward and held out a paw. "I don't know if you remember," the teddy bear said, "but I'm Ernie Fresham. I talked to you on the phone about a month ago."

"I remember," Maggie said as graciously as she could. She gestured at the assembled teddy bears behind him. "I take it you want to perform the Catocal."

Ernie Fresham gave Dunne an uncomfortable look. "I know we told you it would be two weeks from now," he told Maggie hurriedly, "but then we reran the program and we found something we'd done wrong, you see, so it's today or after the convention, and of course it wouldn't be any good after the convention—I mean, we wouldn't be playing by the rules, you see—so I didn't see any harm—"

"Didn't see any harm!" Dunne exploded. "And I don't care if it's two weeks from now or today." He turned brusquely on Maggie. "You can't tell me you actually agreed to let them pull this—this stunt on Bidemeyer property!"

"I don't see why not," Maggie said blandly.

Dunne stared at her as if she'd lost her mind. "I don't

care what we've got written into the L-Star contract," he told her, furious. "If any serious damage is done to these grounds, somebody's going to sue us."

"We're not going to hurt anything," Ernie said sincerely.

"Of course you're not," Maggie acknowledged. She turned back to Dunne. "If I were you, I'd let them get it over with."

"Let them?" Dunne was clearly shocked.

"I don't see why not," Maggie repeated. "All they want to do is march around the main building three times, chanting things."

"That's not all they want to do," Dunne snapped. "They want to burn a goat!"

"Goat?" Maggie said blankly. Then an understanding smile crossed her face. "Oh, the goat!"

"I don't believe this," Dunne muttered.

Maggie turned to Ernie Fresham. "I suggest you show Mr. Holborn the goat," she advised him. "He seems to be a little confused."

"Oh," Ernie Fresham said. "Of course, of course," he continued eagerly. "I can see how if he thought it was a *goat* goat—I mean, a *real* goat—I mean, just a minute . . ." He hurried off and came back seconds later with a large plaster-of-Paris model of a long-horned mountain goat wrapped in strands of colored Christmas-tree lights. "When you flick the switch, all the lights go on," he told Dunne. "We keep the lights on for the whole procession. That's called burning the goat."

"Christmas-tree lights," Dunne said slowly.

"We wouldn't burn an actual goat," Ernie said anxiously. "I mean, that would be cruelty to animals."

"To say the least," Dunne said dryly.

"It's in the rules, you know," Ernie said. "I mean, we're not fanatics or anything, like the Alzibarians. But Ewoks can't hunt unless they have a Catocal, and the Catocal has to be between the third and the fourth day Martan is in the sphere of the galaxy Helsor 2 and has a clear path to Deneb, and that only happens twice every three months, so if we don't do it tonight—"

"Technically they wouldn't be allowed to hunt during the convention, since they haven't met the conditions that would make it possible for them to hunt if they were really Ewoks."

"Well, our brand of Ewoks, anyway," Ernie said.

"Why don't you just go do your Catocal," Maggie dismissed him. "I've got a few things to talk over with Mr. Holborn."

"Oh, yeah. Good idea." He looked Dunne curiously up and down. "Didn't mean to upset you," he apologized. "Thought it was all set." Then he turned on his heel and loped away.

Maggie looked around to find Dunne scratching his chin, a guilty look in his eyes.

"I take it I'm about to get bawled out but good," he said sheepishly. "I guess I might even deserve it."

"Did it ever occur to you that this is my project?" Maggie asked in exasperation. "I've been on it from the beginning, you know. I just might know what's going on sometimes."

"It was a crisis," Dunne defended himself. "I'm always like this in a crisis."

"If you are, you're in the wrong line of work," Maggie said bluntly. "If you react like this every time something goes wrong, you're going to die of an ulcer before you're forty."

"I've been warned about that before," Dunne admitted. "But, Maggie—"

"Oh, never mind," Maggie said, disgusted. "We've had this argument before. I don't want to have it again. I left my car around here somewhere. I think I'm going to find it and go home."

"I'll take you home," Dunne said quickly.

Maggie viewed him with a jaundiced eye. "Let's not start that again," she warned him. "I'm getting into my own car and going home, Dunne."

Dunne looked around the drive. "Where *is* your car?" he asked her. "I don't see it anywhere."

Maggie followed his gaze. There were three Volkswagens, a large Ford van painted with a grinning Ewok and the logo from *The Return of the Jedi,* and Dunne's Alfa Romeo. Nothing else.

"Damn," Maggie said. "One of the technicians must have taken it around to the visitors' lot."

Dunne nodded wisely. "That's all the way over by the Marsh Road. It's quite a long trek. And it's dark. And the weather's terrible."

Maggie frowned. "Something tells me you have something to suggest," she said cautiously.

"Of course," he said quickly. "I'll give you a ride there. It's the least I can do."

Maggie hesitated. "Why do I have this feeling your offer isn't exactly made without an ulterior motive?" she asked.

"I have no idea," he replied innocently.

She glared at him, trying to read his expression, then brushed her doubts away. After all, she didn't much like the idea of trekking over to the visitors' lot by herself in the dark.

"I'll come," she told him grudgingly. "I don't suppose there's much you can do between here and there anyway. It's a short drive."

"Exactly." Dunne grinned.

Maggie observed that grin and hesitated once again. No matter what had happened between Dunne and herself that afternoon, all she wanted now was to go home and go to bed. There were so many things to sort out, so many questions. If only she could figure out what Dunne was thinking about. He seemed so—so pleased with himself. And under the circumstances, that didn't make any sense at all.

She shook her head to clear it. Her life was getting so labyrinthine, she was beginning to see complications where there weren't any. Dunne was going to give her a ride to her car. It was perfectly simple.

She started off in the direction of the Alfa Romeo. "Let's get going," she called over her shoulder.

"Aren't we going to stick around and watch this procession?" Dunne called back.

"What for? We're paying half a dozen guards seven-fifty an hour to watch the place."

"Let me just tell somebody inside what'll be going on," Dunne said.

Maggie stopped to watch him stride off in the direction of the front door. Then she let herself in the passenger side of the Alfa Romeo and fastened her seat belt. Everything seemed so normal, so calm, so rational. Why didn't she believe it?

Dunne came back at a run. "You're not going to believe this," he said as he jumped into his own bucket seat and closed his seat belt with a snap. "They're back there prancing around and singing 'The Teddy Bears' Picnic.'"

"I tried to tell you they were harmless," Maggie said a trifle tartly.

"That you did," Dunne admitted, "and I didn't listen. Not listening seems to be my chief problem."

Maggie was about to say something about not listening to *women* being Dunne's chief problem, but she stopped herself.

For once the Alfa Romeo roared to life with a turn of the key.

"Ah," Dunne said with satisfaction. "That's how it's supposed to work." He swung the car onto the drive. "Did I ever tell you I had a passion for fast cars?" he asked as he swung onto the drive.

"I could have guessed," Maggie replied dryly.

"It doesn't seem to bother you," Dunne said approvingly. "A lot of women are a little squeamish about going really fast."

"You're only doing forty," Maggie pointed out. "And I love to go fast—as long as *I'm* driving."

"Figures," Dunne said. "We both want to be the one who's driving. I should have expected that."

Maggie watched a yellow sign go by on her left. "Dunne!" she exclaimed, turning to look back at it. "You missed the turn. The visitors' lot is that way."

"I know where the visitors' lot is," he said with a complacent grin. "And I haven't missed the turn. *This* is our turn."

He came to the end of the drive and veered left onto the tree-lined road, away from the Bidemeyer Estate, away from New Haven, away from everything Maggie recognized. She turned on him angrily.

"What do you think you're doing?" she demanded. "Where are we going?"

"I told you," Dunne said, sounding absurdly satisfied with himself. "It's a surprise."

"This is kidnaping," Maggie declared, fuming.

"Yeah." Dunne's grin was as wide as the Cheshire cat's. "It's amazing what you're good at if you only give it a try."

Chapter Eleven

"I AM *NOT* getting out of this car." Maggie folded her arms across her chest and stared resolutely out the window. She had noticed the peaked-roofed redwood log structure nestled among the trees from halfway up the unpaved drive, but she was determined not to look at it. She was furious, and she had every right to be.

"We can spend the night in the car if you want," Dunne offered, "but it's really much warmer in there." He tried to direct her attention to the cabin and failed. "Of course, if you prefer, I can always get a thermos and some blankets and bring them out here."

Maggie ground her teeth. "What I'd prefer," she snapped at him, "is a ride to the visitors' lot on the Bidemeyer Estate, which was what you offered to begin with. After that I'll take an uneventful ride home, a long, hot bath, and a good stiff drink, in that order."

"I won't do anything about the ride, but there's a nice big hot tub and a bottle of good Irish whiskey inside," Dunne offered genially. "I may even be able to find us a little dinner."

"Why don't you just find Mason Street," Maggie said stubbornly. "You ought to know where that is."

"All right," Dunne sighed. "I can see reason isn't going to prevail. Give me a minute."

Maggie heard Dunne's door open and close and the sound of footsteps on gravel. She swiveled her head, trying to get a look at him. He must have gone around the back, because she couldn't spot him at first. She looked through the windshield at the heavy forest that surrounded them and shivered a little. If she didn't know they'd come off a major highway less than five minutes earlier, she'd have thought they were lost in the woods.

She heard a noise on her right and jumped involuntarily. Then the passenger door swung open, fingers flashed at her waist to release the seat belt, and she felt herself being lifted into the cold night air by strong, able arms.

"Put me down!" she roared at the grinning face above her. "I told you I wasn't getting out of this car, and I'm not getting out of this car!"

"You're already out of the car," Dunne said, kicking the door shut. "After all, I can't leave you here to freeze or die of carbon monoxide poisoning or something."

"Put me down!" she insisted again.

"Just a minute." Dunne began fumbling with keys, then with the door latch. Maggie looked around wildly. She had to get him to release her.

She tried to kick her feet, but Dunne's arms, already wound around her knees, only clamped more tightly against her legs. Nor were her hands any help. Dunne was holding her at an odd angle, almost over his shoulder, and Maggie couldn't reach any vulnerable part of him. She heard the door swing open on rusty hinges and groaned.

"Just wait till I get down from here," she warned him. "There isn't going to be an inch left of your skin."

"Promises, promises," Dunne said flippantly. He carried her across the creaking wood floor. "There," he said. "Now, if you'll just cooperate for one minute."

Maggie was about to tell him what he could do with his cooperation when an overhead light flickered and then went on, nearly blinding her with its brightness. She blinked, feeling confused and disoriented.

"You did that on purpose," she accused Dunne. "As soon as I can see, I'm walking straight out of here and back to the car."

"Don't you even want to look around first?" he asked.

Now that her eyes were adjusting to the light, she could see she was in a large room that seemed to be filled with shining brass. Brass? That didn't make any sense.

She blinked again, trying to bring it all into focus. This time when she opened her eyes she saw a large kitchen. The walls were of wood and gleaming tile, but they were hardly noticeable. What was noticeable was the brass and copper and stainless steel that hung from every available inch of wall and ceiling space. The area above her head was covered with hanging copper-bottomed pots and pans. The wall beside the ultramodern cooking unit was hung with large stainless steel spoons and ladles. A central cooking island with a redwood base was covered with butcher block and steel and contained what looked like two dozen gas burners, two open grills, and a built-in toaster.

"What is this place?" Maggie demanded.

"My kitchen," Dunne said, unable to keep a faint note of pride out of his voice. "What does it look like?"

"The *Good Housekeeping* test kitchens?" Maggie suggested. "For goodness' sake, Dunne, this is better equipped than the Honolulu Hilton."

"You haven't seen anything yet," Dunne declared. "Watch this," he said eagerly, hurrying to a row of buttons on the far wall. "Blender," he announced, pushing one. Then he pushed another and said, "Food processor."

Maggie watched in amazement as small blocks of wood pushed out of the seemingly solid wall, righted themselves, and became the pedestals of the promised equipment. Besides the blender and the food processor, there was a mixing bowl and rotaries, a pasta machine, an electric waffle iron, an electric can opener, an electric wok, and an appliance that apparently did nothing but make ice in various bizarre and completely unnecessary shapes.

"This is crazier than L-Star," Maggie moaned. "What does your refrigerator do, waltz?"

"It's a walk-in unit," Dunne said, gesturing to the fourth wall. "Actually, it's two walk-in units. Freezer to the left, cooler to the right."

"Naturally," Maggie said. "And undoubtedly there's a button next to the sink that revs up the turbojets and lets us take off for Mars with the minimum of fuss, muss, and bother."

"Don't you like it?" Dunne asked. "I told you I like gadgets. I like inventing them, and I like using them. A few years ago, when I decided to build this house, it occurred to me that I'd been eating in schools and restaurants most of my life. I'd never cooked for myself. I'd never even had anyone cook for me—at least, not since I was a child. So when the plans were being drawn up for the house, I designed myself a kitchen. I ordered all the gadgets available, and I devised a few that weren't. I drove the architect and designer crazy." Dunne looked pleased with himself. "Besides, I thought I'd learn to cook."

"Well, you certainly did it up elaborately," Maggie said. "And did you learn to cook?"

"I don't know," he admitted.

"How can you not know?" Maggie demanded.

"I haven't tried it yet," he said sheepishly. Then he continued in a hurried, coaxing voice. "That's why you have to stay to dinner, you see. I mean, I have everything here—meat, vegetables, the works. You've got to help me find out if I'm any good—as a cook, I mean."

"I thought you said you've had this place a couple of years," Maggie said suspiciously. "If you haven't been cooking in it—and I admit, it doesn't look as if any of this stuff has ever been used—what have you been doing here?"

"Oh," Dunne said nervously, "this and that. You know what I mean."

"No," Maggie said, "I don't."

Dunne coughed with obvious embarrassment. "Well," he said. "Ah, peanut butter, you see. And jelly. Mostly raspberry jelly. Also bread."

The living room was better. It was large—Maggie could have fit most of her small house on Mason Street into it—but it was warm and dominated by a huge fireplace that took up most of one wall. The other walls were paneled, and the couch was a large circular sunken affair with bright red cushions and a center island of fieldstone that served as a coffee table. Maggie gingerly made her way into the pit, then slipped off her shoes and tucked her feet under herself.

"I take it you're not mad anymore," Dunne remarked, sitting opposite her on the fieldstone island.

Maggie scratched her head. "I don't know if I'm angry or not," she admitted tentatively. "I'm a little over-whelmed."

"Good," Dunne said. "Be overwhelmed."

"I reserve my right to be angry again when I get used to all this," Maggie warned. "By all rights I should have your head."

"I know," Dunne said ruefully. "I'll even admit I deserve it. At the moment, however..." He shrugged his shoulders. "I hope you like the house. I oversaw all the details myself." His green eyes grew serious, and he reached out to take her hand. "I've waited a long time to find a woman I wanted to bring to this house, Maggie."

Maggie couldn't stop herself from looking into the emerald depths of those eyes. Dunne looked so sincere, so serious. Maggie felt warmth spread through her. He'd waited a long time to find someone he wanted to bring to the house, and he had brought her. The romantic part of her was willing to forgive him almost anything for those words. She lightly stroked his hand, her body thrilling to the feel of his slightly rough skin.

"Do you really intend to cook for me?" she asked him softly. "From scratch, by yourself?"

Dunne grinned engagingly. "I picked something safe," he promised her. "A couple of porterhouse steaks, some fresh asparagus—I have a built-in electric steamer—"

"Of course," Maggie remarked playfully.

"Yeah, I guess 'Of course' is the right way to put it," Dunne said, laughing. "As for the rest of it, I bought the dessert, and as for the preliminaries..." He reached down to the bottom of the center island. "I don't want you to think only the kitchen is automated."

The fieldstone island whirred and shuddered.

"Now what?" Maggie asked a little apprehensively.

"Preliminaries," Dunne promised. A panel slid open, and something began to emerge.

"Voilà," Dunne said. "Dom Pérignon. A pair of champagne glasses. Three kinds of pâté. And crackers."

"Oh, Dunne," Maggie said, laughing helplessly.

"I know, I know," Dunne said. "But I love gadgets. I always have. You should see the electric train set I've got hooked up in the basement."

"Chocolate mousse?" Dunne suggested.

Maggie stretched out on the circular couch and groaned.

"You've got to be kidding," she protested. "I'm not going to eat again until Christmas."

"I'm going to stuff a turkey for Christmas," Dunne announced. "There's nothing to this cooking business."

"Just remember to get two turkeys," Maggie said. "You know, just like the steaks. One to practice on..."

"You weren't going to remind me of that," Dunne chided.

"You can remind yourself of it by going out to your smoke-filled kitchen," Maggie teased.

Dunne ran a hand through her hair, his fingers lightly touching her forehead. Maggie felt the familiar shiver, the melting, the sudden straining of her body toward his. He was so close to her, she could smell the scent of him.

"It was okay after all, wasn't it?" Dunne asked in a half-whisper. "Mistakes and all?"

"Yes, it was," Maggie sighed. "It was... endearing. You've got a disturbing habit of being very endearing under the most inappropriate circumstances."

"Have I?" He swung his legs up and slid down beside her so that they were lying face-to-face on the couch. Maggie caught her breath as she felt his thighs brush against her own. By moving just a millimeter she could be in his arms and bury her face against his neck.

"I've got another disturbing habit," Dunne said, his voice no more than a throaty rasp. "That of being particularly maddening in the most, as you put it, inappropriate circumstances. Do you mind?"

"Right now?" Maggie whispered.

"I suppose it isn't a very fair question to ask you right now," Dunne admitted, catching her earlobe in his teeth in a gentle love bite. "I keep telling myself I'm going to find time to sit you down and really talk, but this sort of thing always seems to get in the way."

"There's a lot I want to talk to you about, too," Maggie murmured. Her fingers played against the front of his shirt. "There are so many things I want to ask you. And then you get me so angry, or I start to feel like this, and I forget all about it."

"Did I ever tell you you have the world's loveliest neck?" he asked, his fingers stroking her throat. The gentle chafing against her skin made her almost feverish. "Of course, I think you have the world's most beautiful everything," he continued.

"You're always saying things like that," Maggie protested absently, her hands caressing his face. "I never know what to think of them."

"Think of this," he urged. His lips found the base of her neck and kissed the throbbing pulse there. "I meant it when I said I'd been waiting a long time to find a woman I wanted to bring to this house. You're very special to me, Maggie. You're becoming more and more so every day."

"You're very special to me, too," she said. "Sometimes I wish you weren't, but you are."

"I'm just going to have to find a way to make my advantages outweigh my liabilities," he said softly. "Do you think that's possible?"

"What did you have in mind?"

Dunne stretched above her, supporting himself by arms planted firmly on either side of her. Maggie liked the look of him there. His muscles were as supple as they were strong, and he arched over her with a dancer's grace. Maggie didn't think she could ever get enough of the sight and smell of him. The sheer perfection of his body thrilled her senses.

"So strong," she said under her breath, tracing the lines of his arms with a single finger. "So alive."

"I've got a game," Dunne offered, leaning down to drop a kiss on her forehead. "You ought to like it."

"What kind of game?"

"A teasing game." Dunne lifted his right hand and brought his index finger to Maggie's nose. "Each of us has the use of one finger, and we can do anything we want, but only with that finger."

"Hardly seems like enough," Maggie protested.

"No?" Dunne brought his finger slowly down across her face, her throat, her neck. "We stay as far away from each other as we can," he instructed, "and we just touch." His finger reached the rising curve of her breasts and traced the contours there, leaving a trail of hot fire behind it. "You can do a lot with just touch," he purred.

"How do we know who wins?" she gasped.

"Whoever can keep it up longest," he replied.

Maggie wrapped her arms around his waist. "I lose," she said fervently. "I might as well admit it right now."

Dunne collapsed on top of her, laughing throatily. "That was cheating, Ms. Hennessy. You didn't even give it a chance."

"I gave it as much of a chance as I wanted to," she said, nuzzling close to him. "Besides, we don't have time for this kind of thing. Any minute now we may have another fight, or get called out to Bidemeyer, or—"

"Let's at least get a little more comfortable." Dunne slid off the circular couch and slipped his arms beneath her. "I have a bearskin rug, you know. I'm afraid it's not a real one, but I don't like the idea of killing animals for their skins."

"How humane," Maggie said, feeling herself being lifted. A moment later she was being set down again, this time on what looked like a sea of white fur. Beside her the fire burned brightly, and she stretched luxuriously.

"A bearskin rug," she sighed. "I don't think I've ever known anyone who had a bearskin rug."

"I'm full of surprises. The interior designer almost quit on me twice. Designers tend to be people used to getting their way. But then, so am I."

"Don't remind me," Maggie groaned.

"Why? You're what I want, Maggie. Why shouldn't I remind you of that? I want your independence and your courage and St. Stephen's Parish House and the part of you that goes with that. I want you and this house and this fire and this rug. It all goes together, Maggie."

"Dunne . . ." she began hesitantly.

"Shh," he whispered. "I love you, Maggie. I know I'm moving a little fast, but I can't help myself. I love you."

"Oh, Dunne, I love you, too."

The words were hardly out of her mouth when Maggie felt his hands on her head, bringing her mouth to meet his. Her lips parted to welcome him, her tongue reaching for the searching, searing probe of his, which played along the roof of her mouth and plumbed the secret recesses, its teasing touch sending spurts of desire and longing all through her body.

"Sometimes I think I could spend the rest of my life doing nothing but touching you," Dunne said, gasping, as he trailed hot kisses across her cheek and along her throat to the base of her ear. He found the sensitive hollow there and paused, seeming to drink in her scent. "Touching you and smelling you and holding you next to me," he whispered hotly.

"Hold me next to you," Maggie urged, her fingers working their way through the closely buttoned front of his shirt. "Hold me tighter, Dunne—please."

"I can't get at you that way," he teased, deliberately holding her away from him. He ran his fingers lightly, coaxingly, across the silken expanse of her blouse, brushing against the fast-hardening peaks of her nipples with feathery strokes. Maggie felt close to bursting. It was as if she were being filled up with a great hot stream of longing and hunger that nothing on earth would ever be strong enough to dam. Then Dunne's hands brought the white-hot stream to her waist, her hips, her thighs, and Maggie felt ready to explode.

"Come closer to me," she commanded desperately. "Don't stay so far away. Come closer to me."

"I'd rather do this instead."

Maggie felt a tug on the buttons of her blouse, and then the buttons gave way. Feeling Dunne poised above her, she shivered deliciously. She didn't have to open her eyes to know how close he was, how ready. She had caught his rhythm. She was beginning to feel his pulsing as her own.

Dunne's fingers caught the clasp of her bra and tugged, releasing her breasts, exposing them to the cool of the air, the heat of the fire, and the touch of his hands. Maggie arched against him, making herself more available to him. His mouth came down and captured a nipple, sending a flash through her body that made every inch of her tingle with anticipation.

"Come to me now," Dunne urged, slipping his hands around her waist and bringing her close to him. She reached for him and found his chest bare, his skin hot. He pulled at her skirt and soon swept it away.

"So perfect," he murmured. "So very beautiful and perfect."

He stroked the soft, sensitive skin of her inner thighs, going higher with each sweeping caress. To Maggie the strokes felt like waves pushing her already hungering responses ever higher, ever deeper. She clung to him, twisting until the full length of her body lay against his.

"Don't move away from me," she protested as he began to slide down beside her. "I want you close to me."

"I want you close to me, too. Much closer than you are now." He tugged off the rest of his clothes, then slid his hands under the lacy tops of her silk panties and pulled slowly until they had slipped past her hips and were gone.

"I want to know every part of you," he declared passionately as his lips trailed longingly down her belly. Suddenly Maggie felt a burst of flame that started in the deepest part of her and began to spread inexorably to every fiber of her being. A pounding began in her arteries, threatening to carry her away, so strong was its insistent pulsing. Dunne's tongue teased and touched, probed and coaxed and promised, searched and discovered that most secret part of her, until the very heart of her desire was in flames. Then the waves began in earnest, growing higher with each new pleasurable experience, until she was sure she would drown in what had to be the ultimate sensation.

She moaned, sure she had felt all there was to feel. But Dunne parted her legs and settled himself between them, holding her close. She arched forward to meet him, wanting this most intimate of unions more than she had ever wanted anything in her life. She wanted to become one with this man, to hold him inside her and keep him with her always.

"There's never been anyone as lovely as you," Dunne said fervently. "No one as lovely and no one as desirable."

Then the rocking began, and Maggie held Dunne tightly, moving when he moved, pausing when he paused. The waves began again, but now they came from a place so secret, so deep within her, that she had never even suspected its presence. She gave herself up to them, letting Dunne's experienced touch push her ever further into a sea of sensual delight.

He crushed her against him, hungering, and then it was as if the world had exploded into skyrockets and Roman candles. It was a carnival of light, and its music was Dunne's voice, sounding very far away and saying, over and over again, "I love you, Maggie."

Chapter Twelve

IN THE MORNING it snowed again. Maggie stretched lazily under the crisp white sheets and the plump down comforter that covered her, still caught in the web of her dreams. They'd been such lovely dreams. There was a fire and a bearskin rug and that all-encompassing feeling of completeness, of rightness. Dunne was everywhere, touching her, crooning to her, cherishing her. Maggie could hear the sounds of morning in the distance, the shower going on and off and a man's razor humming, but she fought against them. She wanted to spend the rest of her life in this dreamworld. She wanted to bask forever in the warm glow of love.

"You really can't spend all day in bed, you know." Dunne's voice lilted with amusement. "It's a workday, remember? We're due out at the site."

Maggie propped the comforter up with her fingers and peeked out at the world with one eye.

"Come back to bed," she mumbled. "If you're here, it won't matter that I'm not there."

"A week and a half to opening," Dunne insisted with mock sternness.

Maggie sighed. "If you want me up and running around in the middle of the morning, you shouldn't keep me up late," she complained, throwing off the comforter and sheets. Realizing she was completely exposed, she snatched the sheet up again, covering herself.

"Maybe I'd better get up and get dressed," she muttered, feeling slightly dazed.

"Maybe you'd better." Dunne's green eyes glinted. He leaned forward and brushed her shoulders with his lips, sending tingles of excitement through her nervous system. "If you stay in this charming state of disarray much longer, I'm not going to be able to help myself."

"Don't help yourself," Maggie murmured, pulling his head to her neck and burying her face in the thick, silken strands of his hair. "What you're doing is lovely."

"What I'm doing is suicidal," Dunne chuckled, giving her a playful slap on the rump. "Here, I'll kiss you good morning, and then you be a good person and stop trying to tempt me into forgetting our responsibilities."

"This is your responsibility," Maggie said as she opened her lips to receive his. Dunne's idea of a good-morning kiss, however, was considerably less elaborate than Maggie would have wished. He pressed his lips playfully and chastely against hers, then stood up purposefully.

"Off to the shower," he commanded her. "Then come into the kitchen and I'll make you breakfast. I'm going to have to take you back to your house before we go to Bidemeyer, unless you want to return to work in the same clothes you left in."

"You go back to doing whatever it was you were doing. I'll only be ten minutes," Maggie said hastily, scooting toward the end of the bed.

"Excellent." Dunne leaned over again, and this time his kiss was everything Maggie had hoped for. Her arms slithered around his neck, heedless of the slightly scratchy surface of the starched shirt he was wearing under his Irish fisherman's sweater. Then he pulled her even closer, and she was lost in the sheer magic of it. His kisses always made her feel as if she were floating free and warm in a universe without gravity.

Dunne eased her away from him. "Get moving now," he chided gently. "We really do have to be sensible today. We don't have much time left on this project."

"I know," Maggie said with resignation. "Get out of here, and let me get ready. It'll take me only a few minutes."

"Right. Shower's through that door." He pointed to a far side of the room. "The kitchen's to your right when you get to the bottom of the stairs. See you soon." He stopped when he got to the hall door. "I'll make you something wonderful for breakfast. If you're as quick as you say you are, you'll even have time to eat it." Then he was gone.

Maggie clambered out of bed, sighing. That must be what was meant by the term *workaholic*. She'd give her life to be able to forget work for the day and spend her time in bed with Dunne. Even after all those hours she could feel the hot, passionate glow of their desire and the surging answer of their love. Just thinking of Dunne's eager eyes and his hungry, probing fingers made her mind and skin flame into life.

She headed for the shower, grabbing Dunne's blue terry-cloth robe from the chair on which he had left it. If she kept up that train of thought, she'd never get herself into the proper frame of mind for work!

The cold shower helped; so did the vigorous toweling she gave herself afterward. By the time she had struggled into her skirt and blouse and run a comb through her hair, Maggie was feeling almost professional.

She found the stairs and started down them, humming to herself. Dunne had been wonderful, passionate, gentle, tender. Surely everything was going to be all right. No matter how autocratic and high-handed he might be at times, there was one area in which he was more than willing to defer to his partner's wishes—and it made him a wonderful lover.

She reached the bottom of the stairs, automatically turned right, and began wandering toward the kitchen. If only she didn't have to think about work that day . . . She had enough on her mind already. She had—

She stopped at the door. That smell . . .

She shook her head violently. Dunne had said he'd make her breakfast when she got downstairs. That smell had to be *his* breakfast, not hers. Surely he wouldn't cook her something without first asking if she liked it.

She made herself move forward, swinging through the door into the kitchen. "I'm here," she called brightly, a little unsettled to hear her voice echoing off all that hanging metal. "What do I do, write my order on a canister and send it by pneumatic tube?"

"No orders necessary," Dunne said proudly, striding up to her. "Take a seat, Ms. Hennessy. You may have a great deal to complain about in this breakfast, but it won't be the service."

He threw his arm around her waist and drew her forward, urging her toward a small table she hadn't noticed the night before. Maggie reluctantly let herself be led. The cooking smell was even more pronounced than it had been in the hall, and it was beginning to make her feel a little sick to her stomach. By the time she had seated herself on one of the chairs at the table, her knees had already begun to buckle. How could he have done this? she asked herself wildly. How could he have done this without asking her?

"First, a request for applause," Dunne announced. "Is the table not everything you could ask for in a breakfast table?"

Her gaze swept over the table setting. He *had* done a wonderful job. Matching cups, saucers, and plates of exquisite bone china with an etched design in white were arranged on hand-embroidered linen place mats. The knives, forks, coffee spoons, and juice spoons of heavy, old-fashioned silver were placed alongside the plates. Orange juice filled lead crystal goblets. Holly filled a small blue and white china vase.

"It's lovely," Maggie murmured, her stomach beginning to heave dangerously.

"I'd have gotten you a rose, but there weren't any around," Dunne said, failing to notice how green Maggie was getting. "This was the prettiest stuff I could find. It grows all over that stone wall at the top of the drive."

"It's holly," Maggie said faintly. "It *is* beautiful stuff."

"There's much more beautiful stuff in the offing." Dunne's eyes gleamed with satisfaction. "And now, a melon."

A breakfast bowl in the same pattern as the plate appeared out of nowhere, its bottom filled with a thick bed of crushed ice. A perfectly round, perfectly green honeydew melon perched precariously on top of the ice. Maggie had a sinking feeling that the melon and her face were exactly the same hue.

She tried to be game anyway. "Honeydew," she exclaimed, making a stab at sounding pleased and impressed. "I like honeydew. And you've presented it so— so attractively."

"The wonders of the modern kitchen," Dunne said. "You wouldn't believe the things I found in here while I was puttering around. For instance..." He pushed a large object completely covered by a blue linen handkerchief in her direction. *"Voilà!"* he exclaimed, whisking away the handkerchief. "Toast!"

"Toast in a toast rack," Maggie said faintly. "Wonderful."

"Also bacon in a bacon warmer," Dunne said, pushing a silver serving dish in a silver wire stand toward her and whipping off the lid. "And finally—"

"Eggs," Maggie gasped. "Never mind, I've seen eggs before. I mean—"

It was too late. There they were, sitting before her in their ornate silver dish, prepared in no less than three different ways. The poached eggs jiggled like drunken sailors. The scrambled eggs looked to Maggie like some kind of alien blob from a fifties horror movie. The sunnyside-up fried eggs looked like big yellow eyes staring at her.

Maggie started to get up very slowly, but she couldn't stay in control. She knocked over the chair and bolted.

She made it to the downstairs bathroom just in time.

"I've thrown away the eggs," Dunne called through the door. "I've sprayed the kitchen with some kind of room freshener. You can come out now."

Maggie let the cold water run over her hands a few moments more, splashed another handful on her face, and reached for a towel. She was much better, she told herself firmly. Her stomach still felt a little uncertain, and she had a faint ache in her head, but she had substantially recovered. If she could just stop feeling like a complete fool.

She gripped the doorknob, turned it, and emerged into the hall. Dunne had been true to his word. The smell of eggs was gone, replaced by a slightly disagreeable odor of antiseptic. Well, she'd much rather smell antiseptic than eggs, that much she was sure of!

Maggie looked uneasily up at Dunne's tall, strong form.

"I'm sorry," she said. "It wasn't a comment on your breakfast. You did a beautiful job. It's just that eggs—"

"You're allergic to them," Dunne said flatly.

"Violently," Maggie admitted, trying not to look into his troubled eyes. "If I eat them, I puff up until my eyes are slits and I can't see. If I smell them . . ." She gestured helplessly.

"I know what happens when you smell them," Dunne said ruefully. "Why didn't you tell me you couldn't eat eggs?"

"Why didn't you ask me?" Maggie shot back, then bit her lip. She didn't want to start another fight, not after the previous night. Besides, fighting obviously didn't work. She didn't get through to him that way.

She moved past him down the hall. "I think I'd better sit down," she told him. "I still don't feel exactly steady."

"I'll carry you," Dunne offered promptly.

"No, no," she said quickly. "I don't think I'm ready to be up in the air."

She made her way to the living-room door and slipped inside, heading for the circular sunken couch. In her present state it looked like a gigantic red pit, ready to swallow her up. She veered around it and instead took a seat on one of its low upper edges.

"I'll be all right in a minute," she told Dunne as he came through the door. "I just need a few seconds to catch my breath, let my stomach settle down, and regain my knees."

Dunne sat down next to her on the edge. "I could get you some brandy if it would help," he said.

"No, no brandy," Maggie said. "Dunne . . ." She hesitated. What was she supposed to say? That he should have known? But he couldn't have. That he should have waited? But he was only trying to be nice to her, she knew. And she had tried to stick it out, tried to smile and say nothing and go along with the breakfast tableau. She hadn't made it.

She wasn't comfortable with what she had done, either. Smiling and saying nothing and going along with something she hated—wasn't that what she had done for so many years with Ham? She'd ended up bitter, furious, and deceived. She didn't want to go through that again. And she didn't want to start a fight. The situation was at least as much her own fault as Dunne's. What was she supposed to do?

She swiped at the sweat on her forehead with the palm of her hand. "I don't want to fight," she said miserably. "You didn't know I was allergic to eggs. You had no idea they would affect me that way. I'm not asking you to be omniscient. But, Dunne, it's this attitude you've got. I don't understand why you can't just be more considerate."

"Considerate?" Dunne looked confused.

"In this instance the word is *considerate*," she told him firmly. "I don't know what to call it when we're at work. Dunne, I keep telling you and telling you, and it just doesn't seem to work. Ask me, for heaven's sake. *Ask* me."

Dunne shook his head. "I'm not saying you don't have a point," he told her slowly. "I can get pretty high-handed and arbitrary, and sometimes in a crisis—like last night— I can lose my temper to the point of irrationality. But it isn't that simple, Maggie. You could have told me about the eggs. You didn't have to sit there getting sicker and sicker until the whole breakfast was ruined."

"I didn't want to start a fight," she repeated.

"Passivity and aggression are *not* the only two choices," Dunne insisted. "I agree that I get a little overenthusiastic at times, even that I may tend to steamroll over other people's ideas. I'll even give you my word to do everything I can to curb the tendency. But, Maggie, you've got to do your part, too. You don't have to start a fight every time you disagree with me, and you don't have to shut up and pretend you don't have an opinion, either. You've got to talk to me, Maggie. You've go to come out and rationally explain how you feel, even if I don't ask you."

Maggie shifted uneasily. Dunne had a point, of course, but—"When I do try to explain things to you," she said slowly, "it doesn't seem to work. Last night—"

"Last night I made a complete idiot of myself," Dunne admitted. "I can't promise it will never happen again. What I *can* promise is to try, Maggie, if you'll try, too." He slid closer to her, putting an arm around her shoulders.

"By now you must realize how important this is to me, Maggie. You must know it's more than just sex. I really do want things to work out. And I will try. You're important to me, Maggie."

Maggie took the hand he reached out to her and held it in her own. His words thrilled her heart and softened the arguments that hammered in her mind. If she was really important to Dunne, if he really wanted to work things out, what could possibly go wrong? It might take a little effort, but they'd find a way.

"Come on," she told him. "You'd better take me home. If we don't hurry, we're never going to get me into a fresh suit and off to work on time."

"I'll buy you a jelly doughnut as soon as we hit the highway," Dunne promised, giving her a light peck on the cheek.

Maggie got up to follow him as he strode out of the room. It's going to be all right, she told herself. After all, love conquers all.

Doesn't it?

"You have messages," Dunne said, working several pieces of paper from the aluminum scrollwork of the storm door at Maggie's house. He waved the papers in the air. "For once it's not me," he said. "Promise."

"For once I know what you've been up to for the last twenty-four hours," Maggie said dryly, taking the messages from him. She fiddled with the lock with one hand and thumbed through the papers with the other. "Oh, wonderful," she snorted. "Sister Joan Marie wants your number so she can talk to you about Big Brothers. As a kind of afterthought, she thanks me for everything else I did for the Advent party. Mrs. Gilligan wants your address because she just made a new batch of butterscotch brownies and she knows you like them so. Sister Hyacinth—"

"Sister Hyacinth is down at the end of the street, waving," Dunne said diplomatically.

Maggie paused in her fumblings with the lock to look up the street. Sister Hyacinth was wearing a bright red scarf over her habit and gesturing happily. Maggie waved back, turned to the lock once more, and finally got it open.

"Maybe you should erect a billboard at Ellery and Mason and put your address and phone number on it," she told Dunne. "That way everybody will know where you are."

"I might like being a Big Brother," Dunne said, following her inside. "You never know."

Maggie dumped her coat on the chair nearest the door and headed toward her bedroom.

"You can't just try it and quit," she called over her shoulder. "The boys get to count on you. They need continuity."

"I'm not a quitter," Dunne called back.

That was true enough, Maggie decided. In fact, Dunne often didn't know when the quitting was good. She closed the bedroom door and started rummaging in her closet. Underwear, pantyhose, sweater...

Ten minutes later she was dressed for a day at Bidemeyer. She headed for the bathroom, makeup bag in hand. Dunne drifted up behind her and stared at the tubes and bottles she had spread on the shelf near the sink.

"Why do you put all that stuff on your face?" Dunne asked. "It's not as if you need it."

"I have to wear it to look professional," Maggie said, frowning into the mirror. "It wouldn't be very business-like to go without it. It's like not wearing stockings."

Dunne threw up his hands. "I'm *never* going to understand women," he declared. "I was just trying to say I like you the way you are, naturally. What in the name of Pete does makeup have to do with—"

"That's the phone," Maggie said.

Dunne turned in the direction of the ringing. "I'll get it," he said. "You want me to take a message or just hand it over to you?"

"Hand it over to me." Maggie squinted at her eyeliner. "And don't rush. It's just Cass. She'll let it ring for the next three minutes."

Eyeliner poised in the air, waist bent at an uncomfortable angle over the sink, Maggie froze. *It's just Cass.* Maggie dropped the eyeliner onto the washstand and hurried out. Cass was going to kill her. Cass was going to do more than kill her; Cass was going to blow up Daystar lock, stock, and barrel.

Maggie raced into the kitchen to find Dunne frowning into the receiver. "I just told you, Miss Delaney—Ms. Delaney—she's, ah, here she is. Just a minute now." He clamped his palm over the mouthpiece and held out the instrument to Maggie. "It's Ms. Delaney." There was a faintly sarcastic tinge to his voice. "She seems to be in a snit."

"Hurricane Caroline," Maggie groaned. "Just give me a minute to calm her down, will you? I'll be right out."

Dunne essayed a deferential bow. "I've got a briefcase full of work in the other room," he said. "I'll just park myself on your living-room couch and do some of it." He handed her the receiver and strode away.

Maggie looked at the receiver in her hand and shuddered. Cass wasn't just going to kill her; Cass was going to draw and quarter her. Cass was going to burn her alive.

Maggie put the receiver to her ear. "Cass?" she began bravely.

"Where have you been?" Cass exploded. "I suppose that's a stupid question, right? Where could you have been? You weren't home last night. You weren't home forty-five minutes ago. Now you're home. And guess who's with you!"

"Cass, please!" Maggie protested. "You don't understand the situation!"

"Oh, no?" Cass was scornful. "Let me see if I can draw you a map. He was wonderful. He was more than you ever dreamed a man could be. But that wouldn't be enough for you. Oh, no, not for our good old Maggie. You have to have a commitment. Which means he told you he loved you, and you swallowed it!"

"I wouldn't exactly say 'swallowed it,'" Maggie said hotly. "Cass, if you would just listen to me—"

"Oh, no," Cass interrupted. "I've been listening to you from the beginning. An individual instead of a class action, you told me, and I did it. I want you to listen to *me* for once, and listen good. You've probably just blown your case out of the water, but that doesn't really matter, because you can't back out now. The word is *can't,* Hennessy. Do you hear me?"

"Yes, Cass, I hear you," Maggie said guiltily, stopping herself from explaining that she'd forgotten all about the case. That was all Cass had to hear!

"Good," Cass said. "Now, I want you to listen to something, because it's vital. Daystar filed a countersuit yesterday afternoon. For incompetence, Maggie."

"I don't understand," Maggie said tonelessly.

"It's really not difficult," Cass replied. "We file a suit. They can do a number of things: wait for us to show up in court and then try to defend themselves, claim oversight, claim lack of intent. They can also file a countersuit, which is what they did. Against you. For incompetence."

"How can they claim I'm incompetent?" Maggie demanded. "L-Star is the first project I've ever had, and—"

"It *is* L-Star," Cass said. "As far as I can figure out from the brief, they're claiming you forced your way into the designer spot on the game by threatening a suit, that you're incapable of running it, and that it's really other members of your staff who are directing the project, or at least cleaning up your mistakes."

"But that's all a lot of nonsense," Maggie protested. "I never threatened a suit. You're the first person I ever talked to about that. And L-Star is *my* game. It's my design, and I've been overseeing the whole project!"

"Can you prove it?" Cass asked bluntly.

Maggie took a deep breath. "I've got an office full of notes, first drafts, sketches. Of course I can prove it, Cass."

"Thank God." Maggie was surprised to hear how relieved Cass sounded. "I was so afraid you'd thrown out all your scrap paper," Cass admitted. "I could hardly sleep last night. Look, Maggie, there could be a lot of reasons for this. Daystar could be trying to scare us off or scare us into an out-of-court settlement. Large corporations do things like that every once in a while. Just remember that they're going at this thing like a full-scale war, no holds barred. And whatever you do, hang on to that game. Don't let anyone take it away from you. Don't even let anyone modify it unless you modify it yourself. Do you understand?"

"Yes," Maggie said. "Yes, I understand."

"You don't want them to be able to come into court and claim someone else is doing it for you. *Especially* since your relationship with Mr. Holborn seems to be . . . escalating."

Chapter Thirteen

FOR ALMOST A minute after Cass hung up, Maggie couldn't move or speak or even think. The whole situation seemed beyond believability. Dunne Holborn *was* Daystar. He'd founded it, and he still owned most of it. Therefore, Daystar's actions were Dunne's own. Maggie just couldn't believe the man could be so false. Only the day before he'd promised to write—and sign—a piece of paper saying Maggie was excellent at her work. Now this! Of course, that had been just a silly bet, but she'd believed him at the time.

And she had to face the fact that, no matter how upsetting Cass's news was, she believed him still. There had to be some mistake.

The problem, Maggie decided, was that Cass was so sensible. All the way through school Cass had been the sensible one, Maggie the romantic. Even in a case like this, Maggie couldn't quite stop herself from taking Cass's suspicions seriously, even though she *knew* Dunne could never do something like that.

At least, she thought she knew. Maggie shook her head. It was ridiculous. Cass didn't even know the man. Maggie had spent the better part of the last forty-eight hours in his company, and she was positive she was reading him correctly. There just had to be some mistake.

She ran a hand through her hair and started back to the living room. She would tell Dunne she was ready, and they could start for Bidemeyer. They could discuss the situation in the car. Dunne would explain himself, and she'd feel much better.

"I'm ready if you are," she announced brightly as she rounded the corner into the living room. "It's almost eight, so we probably—"

Maggie stopped. Dunne was sitting on the couch, bending over an impressive array of papers spread out on the coffee table. He hadn't looked up when she came in, and he didn't seem to realize she was standing there. What could he possibly have found in those papers to absorb him in such a short time?

Maggie cleared her throat ostentatiously. "Dunne?" she began again; then louder: *"Dunne!"*

He finally looked up, but Maggie was annoyed to realize that he was only half attentive. He still seemed completely absorbed in his work, distant, far away from her.

"Are you all right?" she asked with some irritation. "We're going to be late."

Dunne frowned. "Problems," he said with some concern. "It's the conditions for the rescue of the trapped star warriors. I didn't realize the specifications were so narrow. It looks wonderful on paper, but I'm not sure a player could actually do it."

Maggie stiffened. Then she made herself count very slowly to ten. Dunne must have just started reading her report, and something in it had confused him. That was all. He wouldn't try to take over the game at that point. She knew him better than that.

"No one group is supposed to rescue the star warriors," she told him, speaking slowly and distinctly to make sure he heard every word. "It has to be an alliance. I set it up that way."

"Do you think that's fair?" Dunne frowned. "Everybody's supposed to have a fair chance to win—even the villains."

"Everybody does have a fair chance to win," she explained patiently. "There are literally thousands of possible successful alliances. The way I worked it out, as soon as the players realize they need to be in an alliance, they'll go out and form alliances—some to acquire necessary skills for the rescue, some to prevent alliances of other groups."

"It sounds complicated," Dunne said. "Too complicated."

Maggie counted to ten a second time. This was one of the famous differences of opinion they had been talking about after breakfast. She was going to behave as she had promised to behave. She was going to be rational, logical, and reasonably assertive. If Dunne kept his side of the bargain, they'd get the matter cleared away and she would be able to start on Daystar's countersuit.

Even so, she found it difficult not to lose her temper. Cass's news had upset her even more than she'd realized at first. She gritted her teeth. "L-Star," she said levelly, "made a special point of informing me that their members are above average in intelligence and enjoy being treated that way. It would be worse if the game were too easy. I don't think it's going to be too difficult. Half these guys are even bringing computers."

"Maybe," Dunne said doubtfully.

"Definitely," Maggie insisted. "I designed the game as a whole, a complete puzzle with some shape and substance to it." She couldn't help adding, "And that's the way it's going to stay."

Dunne gave her an odd look, but he didn't argue the point. He just got to his feet and smiled. "Maybe we ought to start for work," he said. "If we keep this up, we *will* be late." He looked down at the papers with a worried frown. "I just wish we weren't so close to opening."

If Maggie had expected things to get better on the drive to Bidemeyer, she was sadly disappointed. Dunne kept going around and around the "problem" of the rescue of the space warriors. No matter how many times or in how many ways Maggie presented her case, he refused to admit that her plan was the right one. Even telling him she wouldn't change the plans under any circumstances didn't help; he seemed not to hear her. She never had a chance to bring up the subject of Daystar's countersuit.

They pulled up to the broad front steps of the Bidemeyer House without anything even close to being settled. By then Maggie's nerves were raw and her temper was near the boiling point. She waited until Dunne shut off the car engine and then snapped her safety belt free with a jerk. She wanted to get inside and start on something neutral, something that had nothing at all to do with Dunne Holborn. She wanted a chance to calm down. If she tried to approach him about the Daystar countersuit when she was in that mood, she'd only cause a scene.

"I'm going to see how they're coming along with the Plains of Qataq," she explained hurriedly as she bolted from the car and hurried up the stone steps. She flung open the wide double doors and raced into the foyer, only to come to a full stop half a second later. It was all very well to throw herself into her work, but what work was she supposed to throw herself into? She couldn't really check on the Plains of Qataq. The work there had been done days ago. Dunne might be worried about their being "so close to opening," but Maggie couldn't be. She'd planned her work schedule with care. There was hardly anything left to do.

She drifted toward the small office that stood next to the coatroom on one side of the foyer. She'd just have to find something to do for the next few hours.

She advanced on the office with a firmer step and opened the door. She'd walk right in there and find some paperwork.

One of the girls in blue technicians' smocks was seated at the desk, replacing a phone receiver in its cradle. She looked around swiftly when she heard Maggie open the door, her eyes widening in surprise.

"Miss Hennessy!" the girl exclaimed, sounding totally flustered. "We—I mean, everyone—I mean, we've been looking for you everywhere."

"I must have been on my way to work," Maggie said, wishing the girl wouldn't gasp and gush so much. But then, all the girls in the blue smocks gasped and gushed. Heaven only knew where Personnel found them.

"What's the matter?" Maggie asked briskly, glad to have something to concentrate on. "It's only, what, nine-fifteen? What could have happened in fifteen minutes?"

The girl made a conscientious, heroic, and wholly obvious effort to control herself. "Some people have been calling," she said. "There are all these messages, and everybody says it's urgent."

Maggie took the stack of messages from the girl's hand. "Kendrick and Holme aren't pressing, no matter how urgent they say it is," she told the girl. "They say everything's urgent. I'd better call Clare Dobson, I suppose." She put that message aside. "And Cass Delaney. I've already talked to her this morning." She put the message aside. Cass really had been looking everywhere for her. Well, she didn't want to hear the news twice, and she didn't feel like talking to Cass about anything else, either. Not just yet.

She gave the technician an expectant look. "Is that

all?" she asked the girl. "I was expecting a major catastrophe."

"Well," the girl drawled, looking distinctly uneasy, "you see, well, you know the transport cabinets? The ones that go against the wall in the Rose Room in the West Wing?"

Maggie nodded.

"They don't fit," the girl said.

"You mean the carpenters brought the wrong cabinets?"

"Well, no," the girl said. She was uneasy again. "You see, I mean, we really did try to measure very carefully, but you see..."

Maggie cast her eyes heavenward. Of all the ridiculous things to happen. Then she smiled. This little crisis was perfect. It would take hours to straighten out, and she'd have something to concentrate on besides the situation with Dunne.

Besides, Cass would love it. It would be just one more piece of evidence that the project couldn't get along without her.

It didn't work out the way she had expected. It did take hours—the cabinets had to be planed down, and Maggie had to do a good deal of the carpentry herself—but far from taking her mind off Dunne, her attention seemed to be increasingly focused on the "problem." By the time she was finished in the Rose Room, she was hot, dirty, tired, and ready to explode.

The more she thought about her early-morning discussion with Dunne about the rescue of the star warriors, the more ominous it seemed. Daystar had filed a countersuit against her for incompetence. Cass said the one chance Maggie had was to keep control of the game and be able to prove she had carried out the project on her own. Then along came Dunne, trying to alter things.

She threw off the smock she had borrowed from one of the technicians and headed back down the corridor

toward the stairs, the foyer, and her office. She had to
calm down, she told herself. After all, Dunne hadn't
tried to take the game away from her. He was just worried
about one small part of it. If only the whole situation
didn't have her so confused!

If only she'd known Dunne Holborn longer, she
amended. A whirlwind love affair was certainly exciting,
but it had its disadvantages. One of them was that you
were in so deep emotionally before you were really sure
of a man's character. She ought to know; she'd had a
whirlwind courtship with Hamlin Marshall.

The fact was, for all her mental protestations after
Cass's phone call, she really *didn't* know what kind of
a man Dunne Holborn was, or what he would or wouldn't
do. She only thought she knew.

She looked over the pile of messages at the phone,
then sat down behind the desk and started to sort through
them. She'd answer her calls, read her mail, and then
confront Dunne.

That would give her time to determine exactly what
she wanted to say, and how.

She never had a chance. First, Clare Dobson wanted
a map of the placement of marker stakes in the south
lawn. The request had come from the Bidemeyer Trust
and had to be handled immediately. Maggie spent half
an hour looking for it, discovered one didn't exist, then
spent another hour with two technicians on the south
lawn, charting the layout of the markers. When she got
back to the office, there was another note from Clare,
this time with a request for some information about the
security guards. By the time Maggie had finished gathering and transmitting that information, it was after four
o'clock and she was nearly exhausted.

She was just thinking she would kill for some lunch
when there was a knock on the door. She yelled a re-
signed "Come in," wondering what small problem had
come up this time. There were only two things she
wanted—food and a long talk with Dunne—and she

didn't seem able to make time for either of them.

She didn't know why she was so surprised to see Dunne standing in the doorway, but she was. Somehow she'd been thinking of him in almost abstract terms most of the day. While she'd been trying to puzzle out the Daystar countersuit and his insistence on changing the pattern for the rescue of the star warriors, he'd been a "problem," a "situation." Now he was a presence, immediate and alive.

He held out the bag in his hand and smiled easily. "Bagels," he offered. "I told the technicians to alert me when you went out to lunch, but you didn't go."

"No," Maggie admitted, "I didn't. I've had a lot of work to do."

"I've been doing a lot of reading." Dunne came in and settled in the wingbacked chair. "I've read your report. It's very good for a first shot."

Maggie felt herself stiffen. She'd almost let herself relax. The bagels and Dunne's easy manner had made her feel that all was well. When Dunne was actually in the room with her, she found it hard to believe that he could be involved in some kind of chicanery to damage her lawsuit. His presence was too strong, as was her ever-growing emotional attachment to him. But she didn't like his words. She didn't like them at all.

"What do you mean, 'for a first shot'?" she asked him cautiously. "L-Star didn't see any cause for complaint."

"They didn't have any reason to," Dunne said. "You've done a better job than many experienced designers could have. That's an incredible recommendation for a beginner—the best I give. There are just one or two things I think need working out."

Maggie looked him over curiously. "What would you say if I said I wasn't willing to change anything at all?" she asked him. "Not a line, not a paragraph, not a word, nothing."

Dunne's surprise was palpable. "What's all this about? I thought we came to an agreement this morning: You were going to tell me what was on your mind; I was going to treat you like an equal in business discussions and ask your advice and opinion on things that concerned you. I'm trying to keep my part of the bargain, Maggie."

Maggie nodded. What Dunne was saying made sense. The tension, hurt, and hostility building up inside her could just be overreaction. Dunne was probably talking about a few minor matters. What he wanted to discuss might not have anything to do with the Daystar countersuit at all. Besides, she could see what he was doing. He was working full-time to keep their bargain, including her in the decision-making process and treating her as an equal. She had to give him some credit for that.

"Why don't you tell me what you had in mind," she suggested. "Maybe we can start from there."

Dunne nodded eagerly, obviously not noticing her hesitation. "The possibilities are really endless," he told her, hurrying over to the desk and spreading his papers across the surface. "With the setup you've invented, there are so many ways to go. You write a very clean game, with a place for everything and everything in its place, but by doing that you miss out on some wonderful opportunities. Now, take the Taldors." He pointed to a spot on one of the blueprints meant to represent the West Wing. "You've got them headquartered in the Gray Room, but they're of no use to anyone in there, Maggie. They have to be outside before they can use their laser transmitters. The Imperial Force, on the other hand, is out on a grass lot by the south fence. You've removed some of your strongest villains to a spot effectively unthreatening to most of your good forces."

"There are reasons for that," Maggie said. "The Imperial Force has some of the most powerful and varied magic in the whole game. It would be giving them an unfair advantage to put them in the middle of everything. They'd slaughter every other group in The Game in five minutes!"

"Not necessarily," Dunne said, grinning. "Now, watch

this. We take the Taldors out of the Gray Room and put them in the south field—"

"You can't put the Taldors on grass," Maggie interrupted. "They—"

"I'm not finished," Dunne insisted. "Just listen, please. We put the Taldors out on that grass lot. Then we put the Imperial Force in the Gray Room and surround them with a force field. They have to figure out how to get out, and everyone else has to figure out how to keep them in."

Maggie's head was spinning. If that was what Dunne thought of as "a few minor matters," she didn't want to know what he'd consider major.

"Dunne, everything you're doing has consequences. The Taldors can't walk on grass; that's in Specification One. And the Imperial Force—"

"We can delete Specification One," Dunne said, eagerly bending over the blueprints and papers that now made an unholy mess on Maggie's desk. He was obviously lost in the excitement of invention, his mind racing with possibilities. Maggie was shocked.

"You can't delete Specification One," she sputtered at him. "You'd have to change half a dozen rules. Even then you'd have loose ends."

"We'll change the rules," Dunne exhorted. "We'll fix the loose ends. It's not that complicated, Maggie. It'll just take a little work."

Maggie felt as if a steam whistle had gone off in her head. "You're upsetting the balance of the entire structure," she told him. "You're turning the concept into nonsense, you're making the game unplayable, *and* you're usurping my authority. It's my project, Dunne!"

"Of course it's your project," he said impatiently. "But I've had a lot of experience at these things, Maggie. I'm just trying to show you a way to make your game more exciting, more titillating. L-Star will be impressed with it the way it is, but they'll be bowled over with the changes."

Maggie stepped back far enough to be out of his reach, far enough to get a good look at him. Her heart was thudding, and her breath was coming in short, nervous gasps. This just couldn't be happening! He was taking over the whole game, changing her ideas, her configurations, her master plan. By the time he got done, there'd be nothing left of the original project but the costumes and the props!

She told him as much. "I don't see the difference between what you're doing and just taking over," she said bluntly. "What if I told you I didn't want anything changed, because it's my game and I want to keep it that way? Because I want a chance to prove just how *competent* I can be?"

Dunne flushed with sudden anger. "Now *you're* the one being arbitrary," he said hotly. "I told you this morning, Maggie, I'll keep my side of the bargain, but you have to keep yours. None of my suggestions is written in stone, but I want to sit down and discuss rational reasons for not making the changes."

"You already said L-Star will like it the way it is," Maggie said. "Why change it?"

Dunne looked thoroughly exasperated. "Because it would make it a better game!" he erupted.

"I think it would make it a mess," Maggie said bluntly. "But even if it made it the world's ultimate total-environment game, it wouldn't be *my* total-environment game. It would be yours."

"It would be *ours*."

"I don't think the court would agree with you," Maggie said coldly. "When Cass called me this morning, I thought it all had to be a mistake. I was sure it had to be."

"What had to be a mistake?"

"Daystar filed a countersuit against me yesterday," Maggie said, hoping against hope that Dunne would deny any knowledge of the action. "They're claiming I'm incompetent."

But Dunne wasn't mystified by the news she gave him. He seemed to be mystified by her attitude. "But of course we did," he exclaimed. "We've got a procedure for discrimination cases. Every corporation does!"

"You mean you knew about the countersuit and you still want me to make such major changes?" Maggie was appalled. "The judge would throw the case out on its ear. Daystar's countersuit says I can't design and all my work is being done by other people, and if we make the changes you want, at least the last charge is going to be true! Do you expect me to just sit still and let you do this?"

"I expect you to behave like a rational adult," Dunne said irritably. "I know the suit's important to you, but it has nothing to do with this. I'm talking about creative possibilities, here. I'm not giving orders."

"And I'm telling you what I think of your possibilities!" Maggie cried out. "I can't take a chance on them. I won't agree to them. You said The Game was good enough to satisfy L-Star—to more than satisfy them. My decision is to let it stand exactly the way it is."

"I can get just as unreasonable as you," Dunne threatened. "I can get worse. It's my company, Maggie. If you want to put this on the muscular level, I can walk all over you."

Maggie got to her feet shakily and grabbed her coat, wanting nothing but to be out of the room and away from Dunne.

"You can change the game if you want to, Dunne," she told him. "I couldn't stop you if I tried. But I'm going to put my feelings about this on paper, and I'm going to file the paper in all the right places. I don't want The Game changed. I've given you my reasons. Take them or leave them."

Then she turned away from him and ran blindly for the door.

Chapter Fourteen

SHE DIDN'T SEE him again for nearly a week, which was largely her own doing. She stayed away from Bidemeyer as much as possible. She worked over the papers he sent her and returned them via Clare. She timed her arrivals and departures so that she had a better than good chance of missing him. Whenever she began to feel heartsick, whenever her resolve began to waver, she told herself she wanted nothing to do with Dunne Holborn or the L-Star project. She'd given him his choice, and he'd made it. He seemed bent on destroying her.

As for the L-Star project, it was a mess.

Maggie looked down at the riot of paperwork covering her desk, rubbed her eyes tiredly, and reached for the lamp switch. All she had to do was finish off the last two sheets and pack her briefcase, and she could run off to George and Harry's and meet Cass for a drink. Unfortunately the process wasn't quite as simple as it sounded. She couldn't finish off the last two sheets. They didn't make any sense. Each proposal Dunne was making was more outrageous than the last.

Even Clare had noticed it. "Are you sure these specifications are right?" she had asked when Maggie brought the last stack in that morning. "These are supposed to be the final configurations, but they don't seem—"

"That's all right," Maggie had said, sounding more abrupt than she intended. "They're undoubtedly what Mr. Holborn wants."

Clare had given her an odd look, but she hadn't said anything more, and Maggie had sunk gratefully back into work. The only thing worse than spending her time looking at Dunne's nearly vertical scrawl was talking about it. Talking about it brought back all her memories of Dunne as a man. It made her remember he had passed out of her life forever, and that brought a feeling of emptiness and loss so painful she was almost unable to stand it. It was just as well he hadn't walked in on her and demanded an interview, Maggie decided. She wasn't entirely sure she could stop herself from throwing herself into his arms and claiming she'd been a complete idiot.

But she wasn't the one who'd been an idiot, she thought stubbornly. Anyone who'd taken even a cursory look at the papers she'd been processing that week would think they were the work of a lunatic. Dunne's machinations had thrown her beautifully symmetrical game into a state of near terminal confusion. His efforts to simplify the rescue of the star warriors had made that rescue—at least as far as she could tell—virtually impossible. His Taldor—Imperial Force switch had thrown the geography of the game area completely off balance. It would take an IBM 3507 a year and a half just to straighten out his rules.

Maggie rubbed her face wearily. She couldn't believe Dunne wasn't aware of the mess he'd made of The Game.

He was too intelligent not to see the contradictions and inconsistencies in the scheme he had devised. Clearly his sole intent was to totally, cruelly sabotage her game.

Dejected, she reached down and started picking up the papers, tapping them even against the desktop and laying them out in neat piles. She couldn't do anything with the last two sheets. If he wanted to turn the Monolith into a wishing stone and make the Plains of Qataq a battlefield instead of a safe haven, the only thing she could do was go up to Bidemeyer the next day and watch the catastrophe unfold.

She pressed her buzzer for Clare.

"I'm going home," she said through the ancient intercom. "If anybody wants me, tell them I've died."

There was a short pause at the other end. Clare cleared her throat nervously. "You had a message," she said.

"Do I have to answer it in person?" Maggie asked.

"No," Clare admitted. "It was Mr. Holborn. He wanted to know if you were going to be on hand at Bidemeyer for the weekend. For The Game, you know. He stressed the *if*."

"I didn't know I had any choice," Maggie said sourly. "The last time I talked to him about it"—she forcibly swept away the memory of that conversation, with the magicians in the hallway and Dunne's kiss still hot against her lips—"it was either show up or get fired. Tell him I'll be there, Clare. I'll show up at the gates bright and early tomorrow morning."

"Fine," Clare said diplomatically.

Maggie switched off the intercom, then started gathering her coat and purse and briefcase, wondering why Dunne wanted to know *if* she'd be on hand at Bidemeyer. Then she forced it out of her mind. Dunne never made any sense. And there was nothing she could do about it.

Cass was sitting at one of the booths at the back of the amber-lighted bar, a frothy glass of beer on a coaster in front of her and a big grin stretched across her face.

Maggie slid into the opposite side of the booth and began to shrug off her coat.

"If you see the waiter, order me a martini," Maggie muttered.

"A martini?" Cass was plainly surprised. "You never drink anything stronger than Burgundy."

"I was trying not to shock you," Maggie said dryly. "What I wanted to say was get me *three* martinis. It's been a perfectly rotten day."

Cass's grin became wider still. "It's been a perfectly wonderful day," she contradicted cheerfully. "It's days like today that make me think Sister Rosalie had something when she used to talk about miracles."

"Sister Rosalie always had something," Maggie said. "We just weren't sure what. I suppose I could use a miracle at the moment. The Bidemeyer Estate could burn to the ground. Then L-Star couldn't hold its convention there starting tomorrow, and I'd have time to quit Daystar before the catastrophe occurred."

"That I can't do anything about," Cass admitted. "And you still can't quit. You've got to see this thing through. But I can give you good news. Sheila Frame checked out."

"Sheila Frame?" Maggie thought she'd heard the name before, but she couldn't place it. Then it hit her. "Sheila Frame!" she exclaimed. "With everything that's been happening, I forgot all about her. I was going to ask Dunne . . ." She paused, pained.

For once Cass didn't seem to notice her distress. "I wish you *had* asked Holborn," she admitted, "because I'll be damned if I know what's going on. Their countersuit is still standing, but it seems to have become inert or something. They should have approached me with an offer for a settlement, or filed corroborating affidavits, or—I don't know. But this is Halford and Long, the best corporate firm in the city, so they know what they're doing. Which at the moment, for some reason I am unable to fathom, is nothing."

Maggie saw the waiter and signaled. "Maybe they're trying to pull something," she said worriedly.

"I can think of three million things they could pull, but none of them requires doing nothing," Cass said. "And as I said, Sheila Frame checked out. I thought she might be a plant, someone your Mr. Holborn hired or convinced or coerced to trip us up. So I hired a private detective and had her checked out."

"You hired a private detective to spy on someone?" Maggie was appalled.

"Not spy," Cass said irritably, "just check out. I wanted to be sure her story was genuine. You're so naive. Some of these corporations would do anything to ruin a sex discrimination case!"

A harried-looking girl whose apron was only half a string away from falling off came up to the table, and Maggie ordered a martini. "What did this private detective find out?" she asked, turning back to Cass.

"Nothing," Cass said triumphantly. "That's what I meant. His report was solid corroboration. Sheila Frame is, in his opinion, absolutely genuine. However, just in case, I got a second opinion."

"Just in case of what?" Maggie demanded.

Cass shrugged. "Someone could have gotten to my man, paid him off. . ." Her voice trailed off. "I know it sounds like a spy movie," she said, "but these things do happen. I had to be careful."

The martini came, and Maggie grabbed at it, swallowing almost half the glass in one swift gulp. It gave her the most peculiar feeling in the pit of her stomach, but then, she'd been feeling peculiar for the past five minutes. Cass's words had jarred something in her, and the pain of Dunne's betrayal and the memory of what she had hoped to have with him was suddenly very immediate. And yet, in spite of Cass's news, nothing had really changed. Daystar was still countersuing for incompetence, and Dunne had still taken The Game away from her.

She took a slower, more measured sip of her martini. "Sometimes I think nothing's made any sense for weeks," she told Cass. "Sometimes I wake up nights and tell myself it's not possible that I've misjudged someone as badly as I've misjudged Dunne, but then I start thinking about it, and—" She shrugged. "Even when we had that last fight, when I walked out of the room, I didn't really believe the worst. But when he didn't come after me—well, it certainly looked as if he was trying to maneuver me into a position where I'd ruin the lawsuit. If that wasn't what he was doing, why hasn't he called?"

Cass arched an eyebrow. "I'm not trying to argue against something that was my idea to begin with," she said, "but you can be pretty infuriating yourself at times. Maybe you hurt his feelings for once. Maybe he's waiting for *you* to apologize."

"Why insist on the changes to begin with?" Maggie asked. "He knew what those changes would do to the suit, what losing the suit would do to my career, my life. And yet, he just didn't seem to care. Maybe that's worse."

Cass sighed. "Well, I don't want to say I told you so, but I suppose I ought to. I don't know, Maggie. You're a nice person, but you just don't have the proper slant on the world."

"You mean I'm not cynical." Maggie wrinkled her nose.

"I mean you're not practical," Cass said firmly. Then she patted Maggie's hand, a comforting, solicitous gesture she hadn't used since high school. "I'm sorry it didn't work out the way you had hoped," she said sincerely. "I may never have trusted the man, but it was only because I hate to see you hurt. With any luck we'll win the lawsuit and at least get that part of your life straightened out."

Maggie did her best to smile, touched by Cass's unusual expression of warmth. Cass was always so prickly on the outside, it was a surprise when she showed the softness within.

"Let's be extremely practical," Maggie suggested. "Let's have a couple more martinis."

"On an empty stomach?" Cass was astounded.

Maggie stuck her hand determinedly into the air, signaling for the waitress. "I need another martini," she declared.

Cass only grinned.

"Are you sure you're in any shape to drive home?" Cass asked sleepily.

"Home is about forty feet east and up my driveway," Maggie pointed out, pulling up to the curb in front of the small house where Cass rented an apartment. "And don't nag me. I only had two drinks."

"Three. You had a brandy after dinner."

"The door is on your right," Maggie said politely.

Cass pulled at the lock and started climbing out. "Take two aspirin and drink a glass of orange juice before you go to bed," she advised.

"Don't slam the door," Maggie said. "It sticks."

"Have a good weekend." Cass grinned.

Maggie waited until Cass was up the walk and turning her key in the lock before she drove on. Even then she just let herself coast. She wasn't far from home, and she wasn't in any kind of hurry.

The L-Star convention started the next day. That meant four solid days in the same house with Dunne—a very large house, certainly, but the same house nonetheless. She was just going to have to find some method of keeping out of his way. No matter what he'd done to her, she knew it was going to hurt to see him.

She noticed the driveway just in time. She gave the wheel a sharp tug and bounced into the rutted path. Cass shouldn't have told her about Sheila Frame. It only confused her, and she was confused enough already. Right now she needed Dunne Holborn to be a straightforward rat, not an enigma.

She swung out of the car and bounded up her front

steps, her mind still on Dunne and the four-day weekend she was going to have to spend with him at Bidemeyer. What was she going to do? What could she do?

She was fiddling with her key in the lock when Mrs. O'Shaughnessy came out on the adjoining porch, switched on the porch light, and adjusted her bifocals.

"Maggie!" she exclaimed. "I'm glad it's you. I've been holding on to this letter all day, and I was afraid you wouldn't be home, and it's registered, so I know it's important, and I didn't know what to do—"

"A registered letter?" Maggie asked curiously. She understood Mrs. O'Shaughnessy's distress. No one in a neighborhood like theirs would send a registered letter, or a special-delivery letter, or a telegram, unless the news was very urgent and probably bad. "Who's it from?" she asked curiously.

"It's from where you work." Mrs. O'Shaughnessy held out the letter. "Ted said—well, never you mind what Ted said. Like I told him, if they wanted to lay you off, they'd tell you right straight to your face. They wouldn't send a registered letter. But it must be something important."

"Yes, yes, it must be," Maggie agreed absently, prying the envelope open with her fingertips. The return address announced very clearly that it was from Daystar's executive office. It was probably something about the suit, Maggie told herself. She pulled out the single sheet of paper and leaned a little farther over the rail to catch Mrs. O'Shaughnessy's porch light.

"Dear Ms. Hennessey," the letter began:

This is to inform you that recent changes in the structure of the design for the project known as the L-Star Total-Environment Game do not affect the requirement, already established, that you be present for the duration of that game. Duration is to be defined as the period between 7:00 A.M. on the morning of Thursday, November 22, through

7:00 P.M. on the evening of Sunday, November 25. You will occupy the Green Room in the main wing of the main house on the Bidemeyer Estate.

We will expect you at Bidemeyer.

Maggie glanced at the bottom of the page. The letter was signed *Marie Hansen for Dunne Holborn.*

Marie Hansen for Dunne Holborn? He couldn't even write to her himself? He had to leave it to a secretary?

Maggie wanted to tear the letter to shreds. It wasn't rational, it wasn't logical, but she wanted to do it anyway. There was something about the way the letter was signed that made her—she didn't know what it made her. *Furious* wasn't the right word. Neither was *dejected.* Whatever she felt seemed to be a combination of the two. If Dunne Holborn thought he could get away with— She didn't know what Dunne was trying to get away with. She only knew that the letter hurt her—the stiff, formal tone, the impersonality of the signature.

She thought back to their last argument with a kind of numb wonder. He had promised to try, and he had tried. He had made every effort to treat her as an equal, to ask for her input about a problem. He had even managed to keep his part of the bargain when she had become increasingly agitated. The result of that conversation should have been a renewed hope in the possibility of a relationship, maybe even a deep relationship, between them.

Instead the lawsuit had intervened, and Dunne had refused to budge. Now Maggie didn't know what to think. She only knew that when she thought of the good things about Dunne—his advice to Sheila Frame, for instance, or the rational part of that last conversation, or his tenderness, or their fiery lovemaking—she missed him terribly. When she thought about the bad things, she wanted to cry. Either way, she felt ready to shrivel up and die.

Unfortunately she had a commitment in the morning.

Chapter Fifteen

ODDLY ENOUGH, BY the time a sleepless night had evolved into a dismal, rainy morning, Maggie was glad of her commitment to the conference. No matter how troubled she had been by Dunne's letter, or how many memories it had called up, she couldn't remain entirely unaffected by the excitement that was the beginning of the four-day game. She'd been to three- and four-day games before, but never anything as exotic and unusual as a science fiction conference.

A large room that had once been a tea reception room on the top floor of the central section of the main house had been declared off limits to The Game and given over to a team of special-effects experts from one of the big movie companies. They'd spend their weekend giving demonstrations of how to make a robot move—on film—

and how to simulate UFO attacks on Washington, DC, among other things, to anyone who cared to take a break from serious game-playing long enough to listen to them.

There were other groups, too. The chauffeur's apartment above the garage had been commandeered by "speculative history" writers, who were giving an exhibition of the technological innovations likely to occur in the next fifty years.

Maggie was eager to see both exhibits and to witness the gaiety and madness of a group of grown people spending four days in full, outrageous costume. She couldn't stop thinking of Dunne or of the mess he'd made of her beautiful game plan, but even those painful thoughts couldn't dampen her excited anticipation of the weekend. On one level her always lively curiosity simply got the better of her.

Which probably proves I'll live, Maggie told herself as she drove up to the front of the Bidemeyer House at a little after six. She squinted through the streams of water washing over her windshield, but she couldn't see anything except rain and more rain. She shrugged her arms out of her coat sleeves and drew the garment over her head like a tent. Then she propped open her car door and made a run for it.

As long as she didn't actually have to see Dunne, she'd be all right, Maggie told herself. The thought came to her as she was dashing up the front steps, and for a moment it stopped her. Of course she'd have to see Dunne. There would be no way to avoid it. Very soon she'd have to stand and listen to him reading off the general order at the start of the game. She grabbed for the doorknob. She'd spent the entire night pacing her living-room floor, trying to figure out how she was going to survive the weekend. Now that she had a partial grip on her emotions, she was determined to keep it.

If she'd been afraid she would run into Dunne as soon as she stepped into the foyer, her fears were soon allayed. It was almost an hour before The Game would start, and

Maggie had anticipated a completely deserted house. Instead the foyer, front halls, and main stairways were jammed. The dignified silence of the Bidemeyer House was shattered. People ran and danced and capered, filling every available space with movement. They were dressed as little green men from Mars, as giant teddy bears, as eight-legged crawling things. The total effect was stupefying.

Maggie knew she would never find Dunne, or he her, in such confusion, and she relaxed considerably. She could spend the next hour in peace, going over the new game plan and preparing herself for the conference. That wouldn't be pleasant, but it was preferable to a head-to-head meeting with the man himself.

She saw a space in the crowd and plunged into it, fighting her way through the costumed hordes to her small temporary office at the back. She reached the door and pushed against it, slipping quickly into the office as soon as it opened. Then she shut it firmly against the crowd. Two technicians were sitting on the floor, sorting sealed, labeled envelopes into stacks on the worn green carpet.

"Are you just starting, or are you nearly done?" Maggie asked, her heart sinking a little as she scanned the envelopes.

"We're nearly done," one of the technicians assured her. "This is the last batch. We did most of it last night." The girl waved a hand at the desk. "We left you one of everything up there."

Maggie looked at the pile of envelopes littering her desk. Her watch said six-twenty. At ten to seven the technicians would begin distributing the envelopes to the players. Then the players would open the envelopes, be given ten minutes to read and memorize the short set of instructions within, and The Game would start. She would be expected to oversee the umpiring, although she didn't think that would be much of a job. At least it wouldn't have been with her game plan. With Dunne's crazy mishmash, they were going to need interpreters.

She hastily pushed thoughts of Dunne from her mind. Cass had been adamant. She could not quit. She could not refuse to help in the administration of The Game. Since the lawsuit was all she had left, she might as well win it.

She started picking through the envelopes, putting them in order. There were one hundred and six separate, different sets of instructions, one for each group or character involved in the game, plus the pink envelope with the general overview that would be read to the assembled players. Maggie turned the pink envelope over and over in her hands. The last thing she wanted was to read the instructions inside it. Not only would it remind her of Dunne; it would remind her of what a mess her game had become.

She picked at the edge of the envelope. Might as well get it over with, she decided. Once she'd read the instructions, she'd at least know how bad the situation was going to be.

She pulled the stiff, formal paper from the envelope and smoothed it out on her desk. *General Order of the Fifth Annual L-Star Convention,* it read. Maggie skipped over the first paragraph. From the bits and pieces Dunne had sent her over the past week, she knew he hadn't changed The Game's objective, just how to reach that objective.

Specifications, the next section was headed; then, *Specification One: Geographical Considerations.* Maggie crossed her fingers. Maybe it wouldn't be too bad. Dunne was supposed to be a near genius at these things. Maybe, once she saw it all down on paper as a single plan, his changes would begin to make sense.

Each area of the estate is marked as a separate geographical area with signs posted designating atmosphere, gravitational pull, climate, and extraordinary conditions (such as hurricanes, tornadoes, meteor storms, etc.). Also posted will be a list of all space peoples to whom the environment may be hostile, how, and why. Area 6, the Plains of Qataq, will be designated a safe haven . . .

Maggie dropped the paper as if it were physically hot. "Marianne," she called to one of the technicians on the floor, wishing her voice weren't so obviously unsteady. "Marianne, I think there's been some mistake. These aren't the right general instructions."

"Yes they are," Marianne said quickly, coming over to the desk. "Mr. Holborn brought the pink envelopes over himself last night."

"Then he didn't read what was inside them," Maggie insisted.

Marianne shook her head. "They were open when he brought them," she explained. "What's the matter? Did he change something without telling you about it?"

Change something without telling her about it? Maggie didn't know what to say. She hastily rummaged through the pile of envelopes until she came up with one labeled *GP16—Taldor*. She nearly shredded the envelope in her haste to open it.

The Taldors, she read in the second paragraph, *will be stationed in the Gray Room in the West Wing* . . .

She let the paper flutter to the desk and put her hands to her temples, trying to will away the headache she knew was coming. It didn't make any sense. It *had* to be a mistake. If it wasn't a mistake, Dunne had done it deliberately—and that was the craziest idea she'd come up with yet! Why, after everything that had happened, would he do something like that?

She snatched at another envelope and tore it open. She would go through every one on her desk. When she was done, she'd know.

By the time she had finished the last page of the last set of instructions and thrown the paper onto the pile she had created on the bookshelf beside her, the technicians had left to distribute their envelopes, and she could hear the drone of Dunne's voice from the foyer.

Dunne was out there reading instructions, Maggie thought. Dunne was out there reading *her* instructions.

Maggie shot out of her seat. Anyone walking off the street into the convention and looking through the pile of papers on the bookshelf would find The Game—*her* game—pristine, untouched, complete. Not one word of her instructions had been altered. It was as if her fight with Dunne had never happened, as if the entire crazy week of insane, contradictory counterproposals had been nothing but her own personal nightmare. Well, she didn't know what was going on, but she was going to find out. She wasn't going to let him get away with putting her through that insanity without an explanation!

She stormed out of the office and into the foyer, meaning to march right up to Dunne and demand that he explain himself. She got caught at the back of the crowd instead. Dunne was just finishing the general instructions—she could hear the words she had written booming across the high-ceilinged foyer like a foghorn—and the costumed members of L-Star were listening intently. She couldn't get anyone to move. She couldn't even get them to break their concentration long enough to let them know she wanted them to move.

Dunne finished reading from the paper, folded it, and put it into his pocket. "Complete sets of the general order are posted in various places throughout the estate," he said. "The star warriors are in place"—he smiled slightly—"although of course I won't tell you where. In exactly sixty seconds I will blow this whistle"—he held the silver-plated whistle in the air—"and the game will officially begin."

Everyone in the room, even Maggie, held his breath. Maggie's heart started thudding crazily at the same time. Dunne was searching the room, peering intently into every corner, and Maggie had the irrational suspicion he was looking for her. He reached her corner and seemed to pause, as if he were checking over each of the costumed L-Star members to be sure she wasn't among them. Then he found her and stopped moving.

Maggie shivered as she felt his eyes raking her face, as she looked into the cold green depths of his gaze. She had expected that seeing him again would be painful, but not that it would affect her quite as much as it did. The sight of his broad shoulders and strong, muscular arms, of his infinitely deep green eyes, sent a pain through her stomach that almost made her double over. Every memory she had of him flooded back, especially the most intimate ones. Under the pain, something else was stirring, something more vulnerable, more passionate.

Maggie shook her head violently. Something crazy was going on there. She had to get to Dunne and find out what had happened and why—that was her first priority. She didn't have time to indulge the emotional excesses the man caused in her.

She started to push her way through the crowd. She had to get to him before he blew the whistle. Once the game started the whole Bidemeyer Estate would be in chaos. She'd never get to him. She charged her way through Alzibarians and Taldors and Imperial Force cadets, not even bothering to notice their uniforms. She'd have time for that later. What she had to do was hurry.

She was halfway across the foyer when he raised the whistle to his lips. Right before he blew it, he stared directly into her eyes.

It took Maggie forty-five minutes before she was convinced Dunne was avoiding her. They were the most frustrating forty-five minutes of her life. She caught sight of him standing on the second-floor landing on the staircase to the West Wing. Before she had made it halfway up the flight, he had disappeared. She saw him again, talking to a dome-headed Mehatibel on the third floor of the center section. He hurried out of sight around a corner before she was fifty feet from him. No matter how many times she saw him, he always seemed to see her first—

and it was so easy to disappear into the crowd.

She was approaching exhaustion when she finally took a seat on the bottom step of the flight of stairs leading to the East Wing. The sleepless night was beginning to tell on her, and although her determination to find an explanation for what was happening only increased with the frustration of her search, she had no idea what she was going to do next. Apparently, if Dunne wanted to avoid her, he could do so indefinitely.

She was just beginning to come up with truly bizarre ideas—like rigging a net and capturing him when he walked under it—when a thin girl in a magician's costume took a seat beside her, leaned over, and squinted into her face.

"Yeah," the magician said. "You're the one. Why didn't you come as a Pterotopeth?"

"I'm not a Pterotopeth," Maggie said. "I'm one of the staff."

"I *know* who you are," the girl said impatiently. She pushed back her hood to reveal wiry red hair. "You were the one the day we held the sit-in in New Haven. You were with the head guy." When Maggie still showed no sign of comprehension, the girl waved her skull-headed scepter in the air. "I sent you a wand," she said. "I gave it to that secretary in your office. Didn't she give it to you?"

"A wand," Maggie mused aloud. Then she brightened. She remembered the wand—Clare Dobson had given it to her. "Didn't you say something about its power to make a man do anything I wanted?" she asked the girl.

The girl nodded. "Pterotopeths are female supremacists," she said. Then she grinned. "We live in a perfect society. Women get everything. When I gave you the wand, you became an honorary Pterotopeth. I figured if you were dealing with that man, you could use a little magic."

"I don't remember—is it written into your group's specifications that way, about the wand making a man do anything you want?" Maggie asked.

"Of course it is. Why don't you go find a costume and join the group? You're entitled. Anyway, it's a pretty good conference."

"It is now," Maggie said as she jumped to her feet and started heading up the East Wing stairs. All her exhaustion was gone. She'd just had the most incredibly, outrageously perfect idea.

It took another ten minutes to find the extra Pterotopeth costumes. They were stashed away in one of the smallest rooms on the floor, stuck behind a pile of Death Ray uniforms. She discarded her casual dress and pulled the Pterotopeth robe over her head. Then, instead of fitting herself with one of the tall, pointed sorcerers' caps, she pulled the robe's hood over her head the way the girl had done. She didn't know if hoods instead of caps were de rigueur for The Game, but she did know that the hood made her hard to identify. The inside was fitted with a mesh veil that would obscure her features while she wandered around the halls.

She pulled the veil securely over her face, grabbed a scepter from a pile in the corner, and started out.

The floor with the extra equipment rooms was mostly deserted, but Maggie had hardly made it down the first flight of stairs before chaos washed over her again. A group dressed in costumes that made them look like humanoid porcupines was holding some kind of dance in the center of the corridor, and five Ewoks carrying a fifth in a stretcher were disappearing down the next flight of stairs. Maggie inched along the hallway, looking for Dunne. She was sure she'd caught sight of him on that landing just a minute before, but now he was gone. She looked around her and frowned. He must have gone downstairs to the caves. There didn't seem to be anywhere else he could have gone. She headed for the stairs, feeling a vague sense of urgency. It wasn't as easy as she'd thought it would be.

A Mehatibel waltzed into her, grabbed her by the shoulders, and knocked his papier-mâché dome into her hood.

"Christine, is that you?"

"No, no," Maggie said hurriedly. "I'm not Christine. Excuse me—"

"Are you an impostor?" the Mehatibel demanded. "There's nothing in the rules about impostors."

Maggie wrenched herself out of the boy's grasp and raced down the stairs. She hadn't even considered the possibility that she might be cornered by another player. In fact, beyond the marvelous usefulness of the wand, she hadn't been considering the game at all. Now that she was in costume, she was technically a player. What if she were captured? The wand was supposed to make a man do anything she wanted, but what if she were captured by a woman? She picked up speed. She didn't want to have to find out.

She rounded the bottom of the stairs and raced toward the wide-open double doors of the grand ballroom. Dunne must have gone that way. If she could just—

She stopped. The grand ballroom, which had once housed one of the most famous debutante balls of the twentieth century, was now an alien landscape. The technicians had done their jobs well, Maggie thought nervously. Even though she knew the caves and rills were all papier-mâché, she couldn't help feeling she had just stepped through a time and space warp onto the dark side of the moon. The whole place gave her the creeps. It looked barren, unreachable, menacing.

She stepped quickly over the make-believe landscape, hurrying toward the far door. Dunne must have gone through there on his way to the sound room. They'd put the tapes and the stereo equipment in the butler's pantry, which should be directly through that green door.

She plodded determinedly toward it. Dunne was a tall, distinctive-looking man. He'd be hard to miss. Certainly she'd catch up with him any minute.

She was almost across the ballroom when something grabbed her ankle. Before she knew what was happening she was off balance, out of the light, and lying on the floor of a very silent cave.

Maggie knew all about the cave. She'd designed it, and she'd overseen its construction. There was a door on it that bolted, and it was completely soundproof. Of course, the walls, though insulated, were thin, and she could probably put her fist through them if she had to, but that wouldn't be playing The Game.

She gave the Dust Pirate standing before her her haughtiest look. His fearsome metal-studded mask, his peg leg, and his curling antlers she dismissed as nothing. The fact that he had somehow managed to capture her scepter made her distinctly uneasy.

"I don't know what you think you're doing," she informed him, "but I'm not available for capture. I'm one of the Daystar staff."

One of the Dust Pirate's arms snaked out, wrapped around her waist, and squeezed. Maggie jumped.

"I've got very high heels on these shoes," Maggie snapped. "The points are very sharp. If you're not away from me in one minute, I'm going to put my heel through your foot."

"Why not?" the Dust Pirate said. "We've tried everything else."

Maggie gasped. "Good Lord!" she exploded. "But how did you—?"

"The same way you did," Dunne said, slipping off his mask. "Or at least it was probably the same way. I thought it was a good idea at the time."

"How did you recognize me?" Maggie asked indignantly. "I was disguised."

"You're still disguised," Dunne noted. "Will you take that thing off your face?"

Maggie hastily removed the veil and hood, letting it settle around her shoulders.

"That's better," Dunne said approvingly. "The next time you disguise yourself, try to wear something I can't see through. That robe thing is practically transparent. I can see your slip. And I remember that slip."

Maggie flushed hotly. The last thing she wanted was to discuss what he could or couldn't see of her under-clothing, especially when they were locked up alone to-gether in such small quarters.

"Why were you looking for me?" Maggie asked him. "You obviously set out to—to capture me . . ."

"Why were *you* looking for *me?*" Dunne asked quickly. "The last I remember, you weren't willing to give me the time of day."

Maggie looked quickly up at him. "I came for an explanation," she said, the anger apparent in her voice. "You put me through hell last week, Dunne. Then I get here and it's as if nothing ever happened. You didn't make any changes in The Game!"

"Well, I certainly didn't make *those* changes in the game," Dunne said dryly. "Didn't you think there was something odd about those changes, Maggie? Didn't it occur to you that someone as experienced and successful at running total-environment games as I've been ought to know better than to pull the things I was pulling?"

Maggie studied him suspiciously. "Are you trying to tell me you did it all on purpose?" she asked him. "You invented bad changes on purpose? Why?"

Dunne looked away. "You cared about The Game, Maggie. And at first I'd made my suggestions just to help. When you reacted so badly and walked away, I had to think of a way to get you back—if you wanted to come back. I didn't think you could stand to see The Game destroyed. I thought if things got bad enough, you'd come to me just to have it out. When you didn't come, I assumed you simply didn't care enough about us."

"I couldn't come to you," Maggie said. "Cass was adamant. For the sake of the suit I was to sit tight, hold on to all my paperwork, and follow your orders to the letter."

"I finally figured out it was something like that," Dunne sighed. "And of course, I wouldn't let those preposterous changes go into The Game. The way I wrote them, they would have ruined everything. So here we are." He looked her over carefully, seeming to search her face. "Do you still think I was trying to sabotage your legal position, Maggie? Do you still think that was the whole point of our last...conversation?"

Maggie looked away, finding it hard to swallow and hard to talk. "What was I supposed to think?" she asked him. "Cass had just called about the countersuit. Incompetence! My competence at my job was the point I was trying to prove to begin with. And you own Daystar, or most of it. So what Daystar does, you do, if you see what I mean. And then you came along and wanted to change my game."

"My irrepressible enthusiasm," he muttered. Then Maggie heard Dunne's deep breath beside her. "A lawsuit isn't a game, Maggie. Discrimination suits are particularly nasty, and they can be brought for bad reasons as well as good ones. My lawyers have standing orders about what to do in case we're sued. You couldn't have known that, but you could have trusted me. Even if our...relationship hadn't led you to think better of me than you did, the Sheila Frame business should have told you something."

"Sheila Frame." Maggie nodded. "Even Cass didn't understand that."

Dunne put his hands on her shoulders and turned her around to face him.

"I didn't come to take over your project," he said gently, "and I didn't come to ruin your lawsuit, either. I'd been working on things other than Daystar for several years. A few months ago I came back and began looking into the business again. I didn't like what I found. You aren't the only employee who's been accusing Daystar of sex discrimination. There are dozens of them. As long as I was safely in Vegas, the people who staffed the executive office at Daystar could keep it from me. Once I came back, they couldn't. When I demanded an accounting, all I got were excuses. Then the L-Star project came up. I looked over the design staff, and there you were. You certainly had the qualifications and experience. I insisted you be appointed—"

"You insisted!"

"Of course I did. Discrimination of any kind is bad ethics and bad business. It's a highly competitive world out there, Maggie. If a company's going to survive, it has to have the best, male or female. But my staff put up such a fuss, I just couldn't handle it anymore. I had to see for myself. So I came out, and there you were." Dunne grinned ruefully. "I knew you were an unusual woman from the moment I saw you, Maggie, but I didn't know if you were a designer. And until I could make up my mind about that, I had to let the usual court procedure continue. It was devised to protect the business, and the business has to be protected. My livelihood and the livelihoods of a lot of other people depend on it."

"But surely you knew I was competent when you started trying to make those changes!" Maggie protested. "I'd given you a demonstration the day before. You read my report. What was I supposed to think when you started pressing me to make such sweeping alterations?"

Dunne shrugged. "I have my pride, Maggie. And I can be hurt. There I was, doing something very difficult for me—asking and discussing instead of telling. I even thought I was doing rather well."

"You were." Maggie couldn't help smiling. "Even while I was being furious with you, I noticed that."

"That's a relief, anyway." Dunne smiled back faintly. "I was beginning to think that was one of my contributions that had been totally ignored. But I was trying,

Maggie, and it was a sacrifice. I thought I was showing that I cared about you in one of the most significant ways possible. And then to find out that you could actually think I would pull a trick to ruin your lawsuit, that you might really believe I was only using you—" He took a deep breath. The pain was clear in his eyes, and Maggie longed to reach out and comfort him. But Dunne was intent on finishing his speech, and she didn't want to interrupt him.

"It took me a couple of days to calm down," Dunne continued, "and a couple more to see reason. But I still needed you to come to me, Maggie. To meet me halfway. I still do. I can accept the possibility that the situation as it stood last week might have been intolerable for you, and that what I was demanding—or what it looked like I was demanding—might have been unacceptable. But I need your trust, Maggie. I need it desperately."

This time Maggie did not stop herself from reaching out to him. "All I could think of was that you didn't care—that the fact that those changes might ruin my life didn't matter to you."

"It was never like that," Dunne said in a low voice.

"I know that now." Maggie smiled. "Although I have to admit, you have a rather dramatic way of proving it!"

"I can think of dramatic ways of proving lots of things," Dunne said with a ghost of his old wicked smile. With a forefinger he traced the contours of her lips, sending a trail of anticipatory sparks through Maggie's veins. "I've got drama in my soul. Give me a minute and I'll prove it to you."

"We're in the middle of a game," Maggie whispered.

"A total-environment game," Dunne agreed, his eyes tracing the curving outline of her body under the clinging blue and gold satin of her robe. "That's really a most remarkable outfit you've got on," he mused aloud. "If I didn't know better, I'd think it was made for you. Nobody else could give it such an air."

"Yours is a little big." Maggie gestured at the folds

of the blousy shirt that hung loosely over his frame.

"All the easier to get out of," Dunne said cheerfully, drawing her closer to him. "Besides, look at all the extra gadgets it's got. Hooks. An extra eye. Think of the kind of fun those Dust Pirates must have had when they went wenching with the local lovelies."

"I'm not going to think of anything of the kind," Maggie said, trying to control her rapidly rising excitement. Being close to Dunne always sent waves of pleasure and anticipation through her, but this time her desire was stronger than ever. She wanted to run her hands through his hair, over his chest, across the taut, hard lines of his stomach. If she remained that close to him for another minute, she wouldn't be able to keep her hands off him. "We can't do this here," she protested desperately as Dunne's hand began to stroke the thin fabric over her breasts. "We're right in the middle of everything!"

"I'm right in the middle of everything," Dunne replied. "You're making silly objections. We couldn't be more private than we are now." He nipped playfully at her ear. "You should know; you designed this thing."

"It's soundproof." Maggie looked about her doubtfully.

"It's also bolted on the inside," Dunne noted. Then he grinned. "Want to see what I can do with a wooden leg?" he offered.

Maggie sighed. Dunne's arms were so warm, so inviting. His hands were so strong and capable. The shirt he was wearing was cut low, and she could see the short, fine hairs that covered his chest peeping through.

"I always did like a man with hair on his chest," she murmured, pressing her ear close to his heart. The beating seemed to mingle with her own, to draw her closer to him.

"Then I'll smear myself with Miracle-Gro and raise a hair forest," he murmured. "I like the feel of those spangly things. They're ticklish."

"Ticklish, is it?" Maggie laughed throatily, giving him her best imitation of Grandmother Foley's brogue. She slipped her hands into the V-necked opening of the shirt and stroked his chest, then reached around him to tease the muscular contours of his back.

"I'll show you what happens to little girls who play that kind of game," he warned her. He tugged at the zipper of her robe, cursing a little under his breath when the mechanism caught. Then Maggie felt cool air wafting over the stiffened peaks of her nipples, and Dunne's hands came down to cover her breasts.

Then his mouth captured her nipple and enclosed it, his tongue darting out to massage the rosy areola. Maggie heard herself gasp and thought with surprise that the sound seemed very far away. She could not draw her attention away from the things Dunne was doing to her, from the pulsing fire that was building up inside her with his every touch. It was like a roaring waterfall in her brain, like a throbbing heartbeat.

Dunne's hands brushed the robe from the top of her shoulders, then slid it down her arms. His hands tugged frantically at his own shirt, and he tore it off over his head. Maggie pressed herself against him, glorying in the feel of his hot, smooth skin against her own.

"Like this," Dunne said, slipping the rest of Maggie's robe off, then sliding his hands under the lacy tops of her pink satin panties. Maggie felt his fingers brush against the most sensitive part of her, and all of a sudden she found it hard to breathe. Her body was a forest fire of need, of hunger, and of response. There was nothing else in the world now, nothing but Dunne's commanding mouth and fingers and the steadily intensifying violence of her passion.

"Oh, Maggie, I've missed you so much," he gasped. "How could I ever have let you out of my sight? How could I have gone a day without seeing you?"

"I'll never let you do it again," Maggie promised fervently, entwining herself around him. "Never."

"Come to me," he commanded. He drew her on top of him, his need throbbing against her. "I want to see you when I make love to you," he said urgently. "I want to be aware of every part of you."

Maggie rose obediently, and Dunne grasped her around the waist, holding her against him.

"Kiss me," he ordered, bringing her head down to meet his. He reached hungrily for her with his lips, his tongue darting out to taste the sweetness of her mouth. Maggie felt him sliding against her, pressing himself closer until the throbbing fullness inside her told her they were one.

Then the rocking began, and with it came an ecstasy of pleasure greater than anything Maggie had ever dreamed of. It intensified with every spasm of her body, building and building until she thought she would explode in a cataclysm of fire.

"I love you," Dunne said.

Maggie sighed, drawing her naked body closer to his. Dunne had found a small hollow on the floor of the cave, and now they lay still beside each other, enjoying the warmth and closeness it had taken them so long to find.

"I love you, too," Maggie told him. "I like this calmness, this being close and warm. We haven't had enough of it."

"I know what it is we haven't had enough of," Dunne said wickedly. "With any luck we'll spend a good long while making up for lost time."

"I think that's a wonderful idea," Maggie agreed. "I do feel the need to inform you, however, that it's not the only thing in life."

"Maybe it should be," Dunne declared. "It's certainly the most productive thing in life. Think how much trouble we could have avoided. If we'd been spending our time in bed, we wouldn't have had time to spend fighting."

"You don't ever seem to want to make love in bed," Maggie pointed out. "It's always bearskin rugs or papier-mâché caves. The one time we were in a bed, you—"

"Don't remind me," Dunne groaned. "I'm going to throw my beeper into the sea. I still think it's a good plan, though. In order to avoid discord, we'll spend our married life in bed."

"Married?" Maggie gasped, sitting straight up.

"Honeymoon in Paris, I think," Dunne said innocently. "Didn't you say you always wanted to go there?"

"Dunne..." Maggie said warningly.

"Just keeping you on your toes." He laughed, and his gaze softened. "All right, Maggie Hennessy, *will* you marry me?"

"Of course I'll marry you!" she cried, throwing her arms around his neck. "I've never loved anyone the way I love you, Dunne. You must know that." She stretched and sighed. "Paris for a honeymoon," she said lazily. "We'll sit in outdoor cafés and drink café au lait and eat all that wonderful pastry and—oh, no!"

"Oh, no what?" Dunne demanded, looking alarmed. "What's the matter?"

Maggie gazed at him with stricken eyes. "The lawsuit!" she wailed. "I forgot all about it. I'm suing you. I suppose I can withdraw it..."

"Oh, no, you don't," Dunne said quickly. "You're going to listen to me on this one, and to Cass. You can't withdraw it, and you can't quit. You'll ruin your reputation."

"But a wife shouldn't sue her husband," Maggie protested.

Dunne considered the problem. "There is one thing I could do," he said slowly. "I could have our lawyers arrange to settle the suit out of court. Daystar would admit you have a case and that they can't win."

"But then none of the evidence would come out publicly, would it?" Maggie said doubtfully. "Wouldn't everyone just say I was, I mean, you were doing it because we were in love?"

"Probably not once they saw it was just the first step

in a major policy overhaul at Daystar. Now that I'm back, there'll be no more discrimination. We'll provide equal opportunity and equal pay for equal work. I'll see to it," he said positively.

His words filled her with warmth and pleasure, and her love for him grew in leaps and bounds.

"But, Maggie," he continued gently, "if you don't find the compensation Daystar offers you adequate, and if you don't think it represents a great enough stride for you and other women, then I think you should fight a regular case. It'll be strictly your decision—for once I won't interfere," he assured her with a wink. "Quite frankly I'm sure you'd win. I've looked over the evidence you've got, and we haven't a leg to stand on."

"You wouldn't mind?" she asked in surprise.

"I wouldn't mind," he promised. "We can think of it as our ultimate argument... and we'll see how well we can do at coming to terms," he said playfully. "So first we settle the lawsuit, then we get married."

"Lawsuit first, marriage second," Maggie agreed.

"Lawsuit second," Dunne said firmly. "This first." He drew her close again, covering her mouth with his own.

Maggie pulled away slightly. "We haven't got time for this," she admonished him. "We're overseeing a game, remember?" She leaned over and gave him a kiss on the cheek. "See you in court," she tweaked him.

Dunne was having none of that. He wrapped his arms around her and clasped her to him, his lips claiming hers with hot desire.

Maggie put up a few seconds of obligatory struggle, then gave him the round.

WONDERFUL ROMANCE NEWS!

Do you know about the exciting SECOND CHANCE AT LOVE/TO HAVE AND TO HOLD newsletter? Are you on our *free* mailing list? If reading all about your favorite authors, getting sneak previews of their latest releases, and being filled in on all the latest happenings and events in the romance world sounds good to you, then you'll love our SECOND CHANCE AT LOVE and TO HAVE AND TO HOLD Romance News.

If you'd like to be added to our mailing list, just fill out the coupon below and send it in...and we'll send you your *free* newsletter every three months—hot off the press.

☐ *Yes, I would like to receive your free SECOND CHANCE AT LOVE/TO HAVE AND TO HOLD newsletter.*

Name _____

Address _____

City _____ **State/Zip** _____

Please return this coupon to:

Berkley Publishing
200 Madison Avenue, New York, New York 10016
Att: Rebecca Kaufman

74

HERE'S WHAT READERS ARE SAYING ABOUT

Second Chance at Love®

"I think your books are great. I love to read them, as does my family."
— *P. C., Milford, MA**

"Your books are some of the best romances I've read."
— *M. B., Zeeland, MI**

"SECOND CHANCE AT LOVE is my favorite line of romance novels."
— *L. B., Springfield, VA**

"I think SECOND CHANCE AT LOVE books are terrific. I married my 'Second Chance' over 15 years ago. I truly believe love is lovelier the second time around!"
— *P. P., Houston, TX**

"I enjoy your books tremendously."
— *I. S., Bayonne, NJ**

"I love your books and read them all the time. Keep them coming—they're just great."
— *G. L., Brookfield, CT**

"SECOND CHANCE AT LOVE books are definitely the best.!"
— *D. P., Wabash, IN**

*Name and address available upon request

Second Chance at Love.

- ___ 07803-4 **SURPRISED BY LOVE #187** Jasmine Craig
- ___ 07804-2 **FLIGHTS OF FANCY #188** Linda Barlow
- ___ 07805-0 **STARFIRE #189** Lee Williams
- ___ 07806-9 **MOONLIGHT RHAPSODY #190** Kay Robbins
- ___ 07807-7 **SPELLBOUND #191** Kate Nevins
- ___ 07808-5 **LOVE THY NEIGHBOR #192** Frances Davies
- ___ 07809-3 **LADY WITH A PAST #193** Elissa Curry
- ___ 07810-7 **TOUCHED BY LIGHTNING #194** Helen Carter
- ___ 07811-5 **NIGHT FLAME #195** Sarah Crewe
- ___ 07812-3 **SOMETIMES A LADY #196** Jocelyn Day
- ___ 07813-1 **COUNTRY PLEASURES #197** Lauren Fox
- ___ 07814-X **TOO CLOSE FOR COMFORT #198** Liz Grady
- ___ 07815-8 **KISSES INCOGNITO #199** Christa Merlin
- ___ 07816-6 **HEAD OVER HEELS #200** Nicola Andrews
- ___ 07817-4 **BRIEF ENCHANTMENT #201** Susanna Collins
- ___ 07818-2 **INTO THE WHIRLWIND #202** Laurel Blake
- ___ 07819-0 **HEAVEN ON EARTH #203** Mary Haskell
- ___ 07820-4 **BELOVED ADVERSARY #204** Thea Frederick
- ___ 07821-2 **SEASWEPT #205** Maureen Norris
- ___ 07822-0 **WANTON WAYS #206** Katherine Granger
- ___ 07823-9 **A TEMPTING MAGIC #207** Judith Yates
- ___ 07956-1 **HEART IN HIDING #208** Francine Rivers
- ___ 07957-X **DREAMS OF GOLD AND AMBER #209** Robin Lynn
- ___ 07958-8 **TOUCH OF MOONLIGHT #210** Liz Grady
- ___ 07959-6 **ONE MORE TOMORROW #211** Aimée Duvall
- ___ 07960-X **SILKEN LONGINGS #212** Sharon Francis
- ___ 07961-8 **BLACK LACE AND PEARLS #213** Elissa Curry
- ___ 08070-5 **SWEET SPLENDOR #214** Diana Mars
- ___ 08071-3 **BREAKFAST WITH TIFFANY #215** Kate Nevins
- ___ 08072-1 **PILLOW TALK #216** Lee Williams
- ___ 08073-X **WINNING WAYS #217** Christina Dair
- ___ 08074-8 **RULES OF THE GAME #218** Nicola Andrews
- ___ 08075-6 **ENCORE #219** Carole Buck

All of the above titles are $1.95
Prices may be slightly higher in Canada.
